Murder at Leisure Lakes

Also by BJ Phillips

Seasons

Hurricane Season

Snowbird Season

Changing Season

Murder at Leisure Lakes

BJ Phillips

Murder at Leisure Lakes

By BJ Phillips

ISBN (trade): 9781948327855
ISBN (epub): 9781948327862
ISBN (pdf): 9781948327879

Desert Palm Press
1961 Main Street, Suite 220
Watsonville, California 95076
www.desertpalmpress.com

Editor: Renwordsmith

Cover Design: Mich Brodeur eeboxWORX

Printed in the United States of America
First Edition September 2020

ACKNOWLEDGEMENTS

Thank you, Lee Fitzsimmons at Desert Palm Press, for encouraging me to write the stories I want to write. I'm incredibly grateful for your patience, waiting so long for me to finish my first mystery novel. I'm indebted to my friends AJ and Mary, who read the first few chapters of this story and encouraged me to stay with it instead of giving up and tossing it out. Kaycee Hawn, I appreciate your considerable skill with the electronic red pen. Thank goodness for your intervention in my apparently continuing love affair with dashes and ellipses. Mich Brodeur, you've created another great cover for this book. It makes me grin every time I look at it. Thank you, all of you.

DEDICATION

This book, as always, is dedicated to my amazing partner, Debbie Hilliard. You inspire me every day, just by being who you are. Thank you so much for loving me, making me laugh, and believing in me.
I will always love you.

Chapter One

JESS HOWARD LOVED THIS time of year. The weather was gorgeous, with the clear skies and warm days typical of an early fall in central Florida. As usual, she'd enjoyed her second cup of coffee in her pickup on the drive to work. She chatted with Walt at the security hut as he handed her the daily contractor's display card for her dash. She called out, "Don't work too hard," and waved at him as he opened the gate for her.

The noise curfew at Leisure Lakes ended at eight in the morning, so at precisely one minute after eight she'd begun trimming bushes on the first lot on her work list for today. A mix of oldies from the fifties to the seventies played through her earbuds and she sang along with the music. All in all, it was looking like a pleasant morning.

In the middle of "Hotel California," she heard something that didn't sound like music—or thought she did. Jess reached into her pocket to silence the music from her phone and removed her earbuds to hear better. There it was—that noise again. She realized the sound was coming from behind Mrs. Bradshaw's house next door. She dropped her hedge trimmer as she took off running, hoping Edith hadn't fallen.

Racing around the side of the carport, she saw Edith crying as she backed away from the edge of the lake behind her house. Eighty-nine-year-old Edith saw Jess coming and pointed to a spot at the edge of the water, not far behind some hibiscus bushes Jess had trimmed a few days ago.

It was an athletic shoe. At first, it didn't look like anything but a dirty running shoe someone might've discarded. But upon closer inspection it was obvious the shoe still had a foot and part of a leg in it. A few seconds of even closer inspection confirmed that this wasn't a piece of a mannequin.

Jess put her arm around Edith and gently steered her back toward her house. Once she settled Edith on her sofa with a glass of water, Jess picked up Edith's house phone and called 911.

"911. What's your emergency?"

Jess thought the operator had obviously been trained to be impersonal and that's what she sounded like—as impersonal as one could sound with a southern drawl. "We have part of a dead body here. It's at the edge of the lake behind this address."

"What kind of dead body part are you referring to?"

"It's part of a human leg. The foot is wearing one of those neon pink running shoes."

"And you're positive it's a real leg?" Now the operator sounded like she was fending off a prank call from another drunk good ol' boy, which Jess was sure she had done plenty of times.

"I'm sure. I'm a retired police detective, so I've seen human remains before. This is definitely part of a human leg." Jess gave her Edith's name as the person who discovered it and her own name as the caller. It sounded like the operator still didn't believe her, although she at least said someone official was on the way. "I'll be outside Mrs. Bradshaw's home when the officers arrive."

Next, Jess called the Leisure Lakes office from her own cell. She knew they'd want to know what was going on when the police arrived at the front gate. Brochures for the development billed it as a "retirement and golf community" for the fifty-five plus age group. They didn't mention anything about dead bodies, of course. That would put a damper on sales.

Jackie, the office manager, answered the phone on the first ring. "Hey, Jess. I haven't heard from you in a while. What's up?"

"Hi Jackie. Are you sitting down? If not, do it now."

"Okay, I'm sitting now." Jackie's voice sounded less chatty and more concerned. "What's going on?"

"Edith Bradshaw found part of a human leg, foot included, at the edge of the lake behind her house."

She heard the expected gasp. "What? Really? Wow...I mean...just wow."

"Yes, really. I called the police a couple of minutes ago and they should be at the front gate soon. I wanted to make sure management knew what was going on. I'm sure you'll want to alert the guard that they're coming. I saw Walt on the front gate this morning and we wouldn't want him to have another heart attack."

"Definitely." Jackie's voice sounded like full business mode now. "I'll make sure the guard's aware first and I'll call management right after. Wow. A leg. Stuff like that doesn't happen around here."

"Well, now it has. I saw it myself."

"You should stop by the office again soon. I promise to stock a cold Pepsi in the fridge for you and you can tell me the whole story."

"There's little to tell so far. I'll try to stop by soon, Jackie. See ya."

When Jess got off the phone, she could hear Edith still sniffling. She found a tissue box and, as she handed it to her, noticed Edith's hands were trembling. Jess sat next to her on the sofa and put one arm around her shoulders. She hated to see anyone crying, but especially someone in her eighties. Edith looked so small, sitting there in her pink flowered housecoat and baby blue socks. Her muddy yard clogs sat by the door.

"Edith, can you tell me again what happened?" Jess asked.

Between sniffles, Edith reached for Jess' hand and held on for dear life. "When I went out this morning to check my bird feeders out back, I noticed a tennis shoe lying in the water close to the bank. I went over to pick it up and throw it away. When I reached for it, it felt like it was full of sand or something. When I moved the shoe, I saw the leg attached to it. That's when I screamed, and you heard me."

Jess patted her shoulder. "Oh, you poor thing. That's awful."

"It was. In all my eighty-nine years I've never seen anything like that! I'm so grateful that you came when you did. You're always so helpful and sweet."

Jess smiled and squeezed Edith's shoulders before letting go of her. "And you're always welcome. The police should be here any minute now. If you'd like, you can sit here inside where it's cool and sip on this ice water. I'll wait for them outside and show them where the shoe is. After they've looked around out there, they can come in here and talk to you. Is that okay with you?" Jess stood up and headed toward the door.

Edith nodded, still sniffling. "Thank you, again, Jess. I don't know what I would've done if you hadn't come along, since most of my neighbors are still up north. It really scared me to find that whatever it was."

"No problem. Now, you try to relax, and I'll bring the police when they get here."

Jess stepped outside and looked down the street. Other than a few retirees on bicycles or driving golf carts waving at her or each other, there wasn't much to see. The Leisure Lakes manufactured home community was nicely kept, with concrete street curbs edging every well-manicured yard. Of course, those yards had to be kept up. Homeowners got letters to clean them up if they didn't. If that didn't work, the park cleaned it up for them and added it to the next month's lot rent.

Not seeing any official cars on the way, she decided to take another look at the leg out back. She approached the bank to take another look at the shoe. At first glance, it did look like it had a piece of mannequin leg attached to it, lying there partially in the water and partially in the sun. Even though the local sandy mud covered much of the shoe, Jess could easily identify it as one of those neon-colored things that runners like to wear. Most of the women who lived in Leisure Lakes, though, were not into running, or at least she rarely saw anyone running. The average age was something around middle seventies, with a few fifty-somethings and a few ninety-somethings thrown in on either end of the bell-curve. Although there were exceptions, residents were more likely to run around in their golf carts than to literally run around. The odds were good that whoever used to belong to that leg wore those shoes for looks, not for actual exercise.

A list of questions began forming in her mind. Who in the world could it belong to and where was the rest of the body? No one had been reported missing that she knew of, so who could it be? Why was the body in that lake? Plus, why hadn't it floated to the surface, and the whole body washed up on shore by now? Quite strange.

She walked back to the front of Edith's house and less than a minute later, she saw a black and white city police car coming up the street without lights or a siren. It parked on the street at the end of Edith's driveway and a uniformed officer approached her. He appeared to be in his middle twenties with what looked like a high-and-tight haircut and walked like he was rather taken with himself, his hands resting on his gun belt. *He must be fresh out of the academy,* Jess thought to herself, noting his extra-shiny badge and leather accessories that were so new they squeaked when he moved.

"Are you the one that called in the...foot?" His smirk gave away that he was trying to keep from laughing.

"That's me." Jess put out her hand to shake. "I'm Jess Howard. The woman who found it lives here. Her name is Edith Bradshaw. She's in her late eighties, so I took her inside to sit in the AC to wait for you. Want to see it before you talk to her?"

The officer was still trying to stifle that snicker. "Sure. Let's see."

He followed Jess to the lake. From his expression, he clearly expected to see something so fake looking that he and his fellow officers could enjoy a good chuckle about it after work over a beer or two. As they got closer, Jess watched his expression change from silly expectation to grossed out.

"Yeah, it's real." Jess nodded, indicating the leg.

Chapter Two

WHEN THE AUTHORITIES FINALLY realized there was a real body part behind Edith's house, they pulled out the stops. They sent out a boat and divers to check the lake for the rest of the corpse. There had to be a corpse since most people don't willingly give up a leg like that. That morning, however, the lake gave up no other body parts.

Jess stopped by Edith's on her way home to see if the police were still there and found several cruisers, SUVs, and the like still parked near her house. She got out and walked over to see a pair of police officers talking to a woman with auburn hair who appeared to be in her fifties, wearing black slacks and a black jacket over a red blouse, a badge clipped to her waist.

The woman she assumed to be the detective in charge pointed to the lake. "That leg didn't walk over to that bank by itself and lie down, waiting to be found."

The uniformed officer shook his head. "True, but it didn't float up to the bank from this lake, I can tell you that. There's simply no body down there."

Jess walked over to the group. "You might want to check the nearby lakes."

The detective stared at her. "Now why would we want to do that, if the leg was found here?"

"Gators."

"What gators?"

"No offense, but you must be new around here. Alligators hang around in most of these lakes. If one of them took the leg, they could've carried it over here from one of the other lakes. Just sayin'."

The detective crossed her arms across her chest and looked at her pointedly. "And you are...?"

"Jessie Howard. Everyone calls me Jess." She stuck out her hand. "I do yards in here, and I called in the...leg."

"Detective Crandall, Beth Crandall," she said, uncrossing her arms and continuing to eye her as she slowly reached out to shake hands. "So, you've been working in here for a while, have you?"

"Almost six years now. I take care of forty yards, all over the Leisure Lakes subdivision."

"You mow lawns?"

"No, the park pays for that. Homeowners pay people like me to take care of trimming bushes, weeding, and edging."

"Does that mean you're retired, too? Or do you live here?"

"I'm retired from the Lee County PD in Fort Myers, a couple of hours south of here. And no, I don't live in here. I live in an RV park. It's barely inside the Lakeland city limits, on the other side of the interstate. It's a bit quieter there, and I like it. I just work over here. Since I don't play golf, I figured paying extra to live with a golf course I don't use didn't make sense."

Detective Crandall shrugged. "Sounds logical to me."

"Anyway, I thought I'd mention the gator thing. The locals here have given pet names to at least some of them."

Detective Crandall's eyebrows went up. "You're kidding me."

"Nope. There's one that sometimes hangs out near my sister's place in here, and she calls him George. He isn't much of a nuisance, really. I hear when they get big enough to cause a problem, they get hauled off to a better place."

Her eyes got big. "You mean they kill them?"

Jess shook her head several times, slowly. "No, no, no. I've been told they take them somewhere they can live in the wild, probably somewhere down in the Everglades. I don't think they kill them unless they're in the middle of trying to maul someone."

Detective Crandall seemed to relax. "Okay, thanks for the information. Could I have your business card in case we need to ask you more questions?"

"Sure." Jess dug into her shorts pocket for her case and handed her a card that read 'Jessie's Yard Service.' "I'm happy to help any way I can. I usually work around Leisure Lakes four days a week, in the mornings if it's not raining. If you're looking for me, give me a call or stop if you see my pickup. That's it out front." She pointed to a blue 2007 GMC Sonoma.

Crandall looked in the direction Jessie pointed. "Thanks again. We'll be in touch."

"You're welcome, detective. Good luck with this one." Jess started to turn around to leave.

"It's Beth. Here's my contact information if you think of anything else that might be helpful."

Jess stuck the card in her t-shirt pocket without looking at it and nodded. "Will do."

Chapter Three

AS SHE DROVE TOWARD the front gate, Jess couldn't help thinking about poor Edith. It'd been horrible for her to find that leg. She stopped in to check on her once more after talking to the detective. Edith was there by herself but said she was feeling much better now that the police had removed the leg from her yard.

Jess turned her truck around. She made another stop at another customer's house, Edith's friend Sarah, to ask her to check in on Edith.

"Why, Jess, what a nice surprise. Come on in."

"I'd better not, since I'm kind of dirty. I just wanted to know if you had talked to Edith today."

"Not since about seven-thirty this morning. Why? Is there something wrong?"

"She's okay, but she found part of a leg at the edge of the lake behind her house. I know it shook her up badly. The police have been there all morning. I'm surprised she hasn't called you."

Sarah looked a little pale as she came out into the carport and sat down in a folding chair. She motioned for Jess to sit on her steps. "I can't believe it. I can't believe she didn't call me." She took a deep breath.

"I'm surprised, too. I was just over there and figured I'd find you there, too. Look, like I said, Edith is okay but the police are still there. Maybe you want to run over there and be with her?"

"Yes, that's exactly what I'll do. Thank you for telling me. My goodness! I didn't hear anything. No police sirens or anything. I'll call her right now to see if there's anything she needs and then go over there. Thanks, Jess."

Jess was surprised Edith hadn't called Sarah already, but it was clear this was brand new information. Jess knew that she would be barely out of the driveway before Sarah was on the phone with Edith. Even more likely, she'd grab up her golf cart keys and head straight over to see her.

Gossip at Leisure Lakes was a hot commodity and Jess knew Sarah would want to hear it all from Edith's lips directly. The story wouldn't retain much of its original gist anyway after Edith told it more than once. Jess knew how these things worked. By the end of the day, according to the rumor mill, several dead bodies would've washed up on the shore behind Edith's house, in pieces. The story would evolve into having the CSI team (like on the television show) sort them out to decide which parts went to each body.

Jess chuckled to herself as the story played out in her head. The bodies would all have been from some organized crime hit. The gangsters threw them into the lake for the gators to finish off, planning to leave no leftovers for the authorities to find. Speculation would lead to dead bodies in all the lakes. Yep, that should just about cover what would be going around Leisure Lakes by the time the evening Bingo games began at the clubhouse. She could hear it all now.

Bingo caller: "O seventy-two."

"So, you heard about all those dead bodies behind poor Edith's house, didn't you?" Ms. Busybody would say to Ms. Gossipmonger as she stamped her Bingo card.

Bingo caller: "B twelve."

"I heard about it right after it happened. I wondered what was going on, with all those police and whatnot. I heard there were three of them, all chopped up in pieces. Poor Edith, indeed," Ms. Gossipmonger would whisper back, after she stamped her Bingo card of course.

Bingo caller: "N thirty-one."

"Three? I heard there were five! No, really! I got it from someone who heard it from someone who heard it directly from Edith herself. It must be right. What's this place coming to?"

Jess started laughing aloud, listening as the fictitious yet close to the truth, conversation played in her mind. *Just shoot me*, she said to herself, *if I ever get like that*. Before she could get to the front gate, though, Gabby Singleton waved her down from her golf cart, her clubs still strapped onto the back of it.

"Hey, Jess. What's with all the goings-on up by Edith's place?"

"Morning, Gabby. Edith found a foot in a tennis shoe at the edge of the lake behind her house."

Gabby gasped, her hand going dramatically to her ample bosom. "Ew! That's awful! Poor Edith. She must be beside herself."

Jess nodded. "She was quite upset, that's for sure. Police are still looking for the rest of the body."

"Oh my. I should go check on her then. You know how comforting I can be in a crisis." Gabby looked up at the heavens briefly before she shook her head and crossed herself. "That does seem to be my calling. In fact, I think I'll go right now. You're doing my yard tomorrow, right?"

"As usual, Gabby. I'll be there." Before the last word left Jess' lips, Gabby had put her golf cart in gear and pulled away. "See ya," Jess hollered after her. She shook her head slowly as she watched Gabby's golf cart drive off. *And the vultures are gathering now*, Jess thought.

Chapter Four

THE NEXT MORNING, WHILE trimming Irene Watson's bougainvillea vines, Jess was regaled with a blow by blow retelling of last night's Bingo game. Irene, another octogenarian, avid Bingo player, and just as avid gossip repeater, appeared hardly able to wait for Jess to get there. She came out immediately to hang around while Jess worked, going on and on about who won, who lost, who threw a fit, and the big story about 'Edith's Leg,' as it was now called.

"I heard you were there when it happened," Irene said, wanting more scuttlebutt ammunition. She'd come out into her yard in her housecoat and slippers, coffee mug in one hand and cigarette in the other.

"I was there right after Edith found it, if that's what you mean, not when the leg showed up."

"Do you have any idea how long it had been there?" Irene took another drag from her cigarette as she took another half-step closer.

"Edith fills her bird feeder every couple of days, and I was just there a couple of days ago myself, trimming the hibiscus bush next to the lake. It wasn't there then, obviously. Other than that, I've no idea when it got there or how."

"Poor Edith. She must've screamed like crazy when she saw that."

"She did, as most people would. I heard her and I came running from the snowbird's house next door. That's all I know." Jess tried to move farther away from Irene's cigarette smoke.

Irene merely took a step to stand closer. "Edith said you talked to the detective. Did you find out anything?"

Jess coughed as she pointed her finger at Irene's smoke and moved away again. "No, they're going to look in the other lakes near there. You know, the gators and all..."

Irene finally took the hint. She put out the cigarette. "Oh, sorry. Collette over on Sunlit Way said the police were out in the lake behind her house yesterday afternoon with a boat and divers. Guess they were still looking for more bodies, then."

"More bodies or more body parts? Only one leg was found behind Edith's."

"But I heard..."

"Well, you heard wrong. You can't believe everything you hear around here, you know."

Irene sighed. Her disappointment obvious from her slumped shoulders.

"Isn't one body bad enough? Seriously, Irene..." Jess turned her attention back to the bougainvillea. While the flowers on that vine were gorgeous, its thorns were definite attention-grabbers, even while wearing heavy leather gloves.

"I'm sorry. I guess I got carried away. You probably saw dead bodies all the time when you were with the police, but it's a big deal here. It's got everyone spooked."

Jess turned back around to face her, pointing her clippers at her as she spoke. "Irene, how many years have you lived here?"

"Ten or eleven, by now. Why?"

"Has anything like this ever happened here before?"

"No, at least not while I've been living here."

"Haven't you always felt safe living here?"

Irene shifted from one foot to the other as she considered it. "Yes, I guess I have. We do have gates and a security guard."

Jess pointed her clippers at her again. "Okay, then. That means you probably don't need to worry too much about this. It'll all get sorted out." She turned back to the vines.

"Well, it's a possibility that maybe I watch too many police shows on TV. I've been going through all of this in my head though, and I'm thinking it has to be someone who lives here."

"Someone who..."

Irene waved her hand around. "You know, the leg."

"Oh. Yes, I'd say so, too."

"Well, don't you think someone should be reported missing by now?"

Jess turned to regard Irene. "Come to think of it, you're probably right." She thought for a few seconds. "Nobody's been reported missing yet. It could be a snowbird then." For some reason, Jess knew it wasn't one of them as soon as she said it.

"I guess it's possible," Irene said. "Those winter people barely started coming back last week. Don't you think someone would've noticed?"

Jess shrugged. "It's conceivable, anyway. Listen, I'm sure the detectives are doing their best to figure this out. I hear they don't like unsolved crimes on their books, especially ones with severed limbs."

A little smile crossed Irene's face. "I guess so. This thing was the lead story on the news last night. They didn't mention a bunch of bodies either, so I guess that was just gossip. Some of us thought they didn't want to start a panic and that's why they didn't mention the other bodies."

Jess lowered her clippers and looked straight at her. "Irene, think a minute. Since when has the news media missed jumping right onto a splashy story? Don't you think that if there were multiple bodies found that they would've been on it like stink on a bug?"

Irene sighed. "Yes, I'm sure you're right. Didn't you see the news last night?"

Jess took off her hat and wiped her brow with the back of her arm. "No, I didn't. I try not to watch much of the news nowadays, to tell you the truth. Why?"

"Well, because of this whole incident here, for one. Didn't you want to know what was going on?"

"Not really." Jess sighed, looking at the bougainvillea and then back at Irene. "Right now I admit I'm becoming a bit intrigued. I do wonder who it could be in the lake, I mean." Jess put her hat back on. "I imagine the body was probably someone who lives here, but it sure seems odd no one has been reported missing."

"Well, the latest story going around is that they think George did it."

"What? George? What did he have to do with it?"

"Well, you know...a leg dragged up toward the shore. They think it's possible that George..."

Jess pursed her lips and shook her head slowly. "I don't think so. George is more into birds and the like. Now if it was part of a dead duck, maybe."

"Well, if George did do it, you know they'll hunt him and put him down."

"And you and I both know he'd be easy to find."

"Yep. Sunning himself on the edge of the lake near the clubhouse."

Chapter Five

JESS HAD DECIDED SHE was going to try to stay out of the whole thing surrounding the Leisure Lakes Murder, as it was now being called. She wasn't a police detective anymore, and she didn't want to be. As much as she loved it, that job had cost her way too many sleepless nights and every relationship she'd ever had. She was happy now, taking care of other people's bushes, killing weeds, laying mulch, and doing the edging. She didn't need to get wound up about something that, when it came right down to it, had nothing to do with her. At least, that's what she kept telling herself.

A couple of days after the 'Edith's Leg' incident, Jess was sitting on her tailgate, taking a break between yards when her phone rang. She didn't even look at the caller ID window to see who it was, expecting it to be one of her customers asking for her to put down mulch or some such.

A cheery voice on the other end said, "Good morning, is this Jessie's Yard Service? Detective Crandall here. Beth. I hope I didn't interrupt anything."

Detective Crandall–Beth–sounded much less official today than when they last spoke. "Good morning, Beth. I'm taking a little water break, so you're not bothering me at all. What can I do for you?"

"I'll buy you a cup of coffee wherever you like if you'll give me some of your time."

"I'll be happy to help any way I can."

"As you guessed, I'm new here and could use your experience working at Leisure Lakes. I'd like to pick your brain about the place and its residents. When do you think you could be available?"

"I have one more yard to do and if you give me time to get cleaned up, I can be available in about an hour and a half."

"Let's make it lunch, then. My treat. Wherever you say."

"Oh, you don't need to do that. I don't mind talking shop with you, though."

"I insist. It would be my pleasure. Where would you like to go?"

"All right, how about the Steak and Shake over on Highway 98? It shouldn't be too busy, especially on a weekday."

"Works for me. See you at eleven-thirty then."

After she hung up, Jess tried to remember the last time she'd had a sit-down meal with someone who wasn't old enough to be her mother or young enough to be her child, if she'd ever had any. She knew it'd been a while. No matter. At least Detective Crandall—Beth, she reminded herself—might be a more interesting meal companion than she was used to. And if she remembered correctly, she'd be a rather nice-looking one, to boot.

Don't go there, her brain warned. *You've had nothing but trouble getting involved with others of the blue persuasion. Besides, she's probably got a huge hulk of a boyfriend or husband and simply wants information, like she says. Enjoy the free lunch, help her out, and then leave it alone.*

Her curiosity was well in gear when eleven-thirty arrived and Detective Beth, or DB in her mind, came walking up to where Jess waited in front of the Steak and Shake. This time she paid more attention, noticing Beth was quite attractive and appeared to be in her early to middle fifties. Her auburn hair with the beginnings of silver streaks was pulled back into a neat knot at the nape of her neck. She knew she shouldn't be giving her a cute nickname like DB. Beth. Just Beth, she reminded herself.

"Thanks for coming." Beth extended her hand in greeting.

Jess exchanged handshakes. "No problem. Glad to be of help."

Within minutes, they were seated in a booth near the window and had ordered their double-steakburgers-with-cheese combos. Beth had a coupon for a deal on two of them. The waitress had already returned with their sodas and left them alone.

"So, do you always carry coupons in your jacket pocket, just in case?"

Beth laughed. "Not usually. Since I knew I was coming here, I stopped at home and grabbed them off the fridge. It was on my way and there was no sense in wasting them."

Jess removed the paper wrapper from her straw and stuck it in her Coke. "Wouldn't you rather use them taking your husband to lunch? Guys seem to love this place and its steakburgers."

"No husband. Not my thing. So, tell me again about how long you've been working out there at Leisure Lakes and what you do." Beth took out a small pad and pen.

Jess noted how fast she changed the subject. "Six years now. I trim my customers' bushes, edge the grass along the driveways and the street in front of their homes, and get rid of weeds. I sometimes lay mulch for my customers, too. The park pays for mowing and I do most everything else. My turn. How long have you been with Lakeland Police?"

Beth smiled. "Fair enough. I've only been here for three months. Seems like even less."

Jess nodded. "I kind of thought so. If you don't mind my asking, where'd you come from? I'm merely curious."

"That's two questions." Beth grinned. "I don't mind at all. I came here from New York. Not the city, a place you've probably never heard of."

"Try me." Jess grinned back and took a sip from her Coke.

"Okay, it's in Cattaraugus County in upstate New York. I was with the Olean Investigations Unit."

Jess' eyebrows went up. "Really? One of my snowbird customers comes down from Olean every year. She says although the area's gorgeous, the winters there are beautiful but nasty."

Beth nodded. "I'd call that an accurate description. That's what finally drove me away from there. I got tired of the months of snow, then the dirty slush. Anyway, let's talk Leisure Lakes."

"Sure. I'll tell you anything that you want to know. Couldn't you have gotten better information from the sales office, though? Jackie's the office administrator, and Chris is the sales manager. Between them, they know nearly everything about that place. What they don't know, Butch Grayson would. He's in charge of the entire subdivision."

"Yes, maybe. I talked to Chris and got a lot of stuff about how long the place has been open, how many homes they plan to build in the development, and how many are available for sale. You, on the other hand, know a lot of the people who live there. They talk to you, and I'll bet they even tell you the local gossip, too."

Jess nodded slowly as she shrugged her shoulders. "I hear more than I want to hear, to tell you the truth. The rumor mill works overtime at Leisure Lakes, like in a lot of retirement communities. Everyone loves to tell me what they know, hoping I've heard something else they can pass along." She paused and grinned. "I listen, but I don't repeat it."

"Okay, then what are you hearing right now about that incident you reported?"

"The leg thing? Mostly that the locals have blown it way out of proportion. They're sure there were several bodies and that CSI, like on the television show, has been out there." Jess put her finger up. "Oh, and one more thing. The latest is that it's an organized crime hit—that's my favorite."

Beth rolled her pretty green eyes and shook her head. "Good Lord, they sure have active imaginations, don't they? Or could it be they also watch way too many of those TV police and mystery shows?"

Uh oh, did I just think 'pretty' green eyes? Jess shook her head to clear her mind. "Who knows? I've been trying to squash whatever I hear, although you know how that goes."

"Have you heard anything about anyone missing?"

"Surprisingly, no. I'm rather surprised that no one I've talked to is even speculating about the dead person's identity. It looked like a woman's shoe. I think she probably isn't a snowbird since they've barely started to arrive. More than likely, it's going to be someone who lives here year-round. You haven't had any leads at all on that?"

Beth put her pen down. "No, we haven't. You'd think someone would've been reported missing by now, unless they live alone, and no one has noticed they're not out and about."

Jess pursed her lips and thought. "Even if they live alone, neighbors there are nosy enough to notice if they don't see them for several days. If no one has been in or out of a house and the newspapers start piling up, it would be noticed, believe me."

"One would think." Beth shrugged. "Well, here's my take on it: someone is obviously not there, but perhaps no one has reported them missing on purpose. I mean really, how many women—and you're right, it's a woman's leg, by the way—run around in those neon pink running shoes? Someone must've seen her, but so far no one is saying anything."

"Fascinating. Those shoes certainly are an eye-catcher."

Beth leaned forward, her crossed arms on the table. "Here's what I have in mind if you're willing. I know you've got to be all over that place with your yard business. If you hear anything at all that might lead us somewhere—anywhere—on this, please let me know. It's been a couple of days now, and my boss will be on my ass soon about this one."

"I bet. Something like that doesn't happen around here. If someone's murdered, they usually stab or shoot them or something, not cut their leg off."

"To tell you the truth, that isn't a fully accurate description of what we found."

"No? What was it, then?"

"It appears to have been bitten off or at least chewed on by an alligator."

"Wow. I'm surprised. I didn't see the whole thing, and quite frankly, I didn't want to. I suppose you checked the hospitals for someone coming in without a lower leg, right?"

Beth laughed, a pleasant sound to Jess' ear. "I did. So the rest of the woman has to be somewhere."

"Very true."

Beth's phone went off just then. Jess heard her say, "Really?" and "I'll be there shortly" to whoever she was talking to. When the call ended, Beth looked around for the waitress as she said to Jess, "That was the search party. They found the rest of the body."

"Where was it?"

"Over in that big lake by the clubhouse. Hang on." She finally flagged down the waitress and asked for their meals to go. "I hope you don't mind. I thought maybe you'd like to see the outcome of your report."

Jess shook her head. "I don't mind at all. I'm good at eating in my truck."

Chapter Six

JESS FOLLOWED BETH BACK to Leisure Lakes as she munched on her cheeseburger and fries. She was sorry their lunch was interrupted but she'd heard enough to decide that Beth could be an interesting person and could possibly become a friend. It might be fun to talk shop again with someone, especially with someone that looked like Beth. *Just friends*, the other side of her brain reminded her.

As they pulled into the Leisure Lakes front gate, Jess wadded up the cheeseburger wrapper and shoved her last French fry in her mouth. Grant, that afternoon's security guard, waved the detective through without slowing her down much. He then gave Jess a little bit of a hard time about following cute cops around before giving her a visitor's card for her dash and lifting the gate.

By the time Grant let Jess in, Beth was already several blocks ahead of her. Jess knew the way to the clubhouse. It sat on a natural lake near the center of the sprawling subdivision. The residents loved that lake and several of her customers owned small boats and fishing gear they used year-round to try their luck on the stocked fish. She'd seen others fishing from the pier behind the clubhouse or from the lakeside, always keeping an eye out for the resident alligators.

As Jess pulled up behind the detective's SUV, a uniformed officer appeared at the door of her truck as Jess shut the engine off.

"Are you Jessie Howard?" he asked her.

She pulled out her ID. "That would be me," she said as the officer looked at her driver's license.

"Detective Crandall asked me to escort you to her. Please don't touch anything or go anywhere else in that area."

"No problem. Lead the way."

Well now, that was great of Beth, Jess thought. She didn't have any official status and was not supposed to be inside the crime tape area. She was starting to feel like one of her TV heroes, Jessica Fletcher—or JB Fletcher—from the eighties and nineties series *Murder, She Wrote*. That comparison made her realize she was showing her age for sure.

She was still grinning and chuckling to herself when she reached

Beth. What she saw next made her quit grinning and stop dead in her tracks. They had a body all right, laid out on the grassy bank of the lake, covered with a lightweight tarp. From the outline of it, the body was missing part of the left leg—the same part that had shown up behind Edith's house.

Standing a few feet away from the tarp-covered body was Butch Grayson. His real name was Jim, but Jess had never heard anyone call him that. She wasn't surprised to see him there, since he was the Leisure Lakes manager. She was, however, surprised to see him that upset. As the manager, he was always smiling and shaking hands with people, but she'd rarely seen him show much of anything she would call real emotion. He looked like he was in actual distress. Of course, once the word got out that something like that happened at Leisure Lakes, he was going to catch hell from the big bosses just because they needed to blame someone for the bad press. That could explain why he was so agitated.

Jess leaned toward Beth to ask who the body was. She opened her mouth, but before she could get a word out, one of the officers pulled back the tarp for Butch to see who it was. Butch's face turned white so fast you'd think someone pulled the drain plug on all his blood. Jess caught a glimpse of the body under the tarp and knew immediately who it was—Butch's wife, Rita. He dropped to his knees and looked like he was about to pass out when two officers helped him up and walked him away to sit in the clubhouse.

She couldn't think of a single person who liked Rita. Even her cronies didn't really like her, from all the tales that went around about her. They put up with her because she was Butch's wife and they liked to be seen with her. Behind her back, they talked about her constantly—and not in a nice way. Again, that's only what she'd heard.

"Did you know the dead woman?" Beth asked Jess in a monotone, without taking her eyes off the crime scene.

Jess shook her head. "Not really, since I don't do their yard. I know who she is, though."

"She's his wife."

"Right. I knew that. I meant I've never talked to her. I've simply seen her around and heard gossip from my customers about her."

Beth nodded and whispered, "Okay, it looks like we need to talk some more. I need to know what you know. Sometimes you find out more through the local chat line than at the actual crime scene."

Jess shrugged. "That can be true, depending on the group. Here, it's a definite. This place runs on hearsay. If you want to catch a bunch of it, just show up at the weekly Bingo game or card games or potlucks—all at the clubhouse."

"I don't know how much they'd talk to me. You, though..." Beth raised her eyebrows and tilted her head as she grinned at Jess.

Jess shook her head. "Oh, come on now. I'm sure the manager can get you in to talk to them, especially since it's his wife that's dead. Believe me, the locals would love to get their chance to talk to a real live detective. They'd get a chance to find out the low down on what's happening—as much as you're inclined to tell them and ask all kinds of gruesome questions. By the way, I heard they had a potluck here in the clubhouse just a few days ago. You may want to ask for a copy of the last sign-up sheet. If they're like the place I live in, you sign up with your name and lot number and what you're going to bring. That, at least, would give you a start on who was at the last event here. Never know what they might have seen."

"Okay, fine. Thanks for the help." Beth pointed her finger at Jess. "You still owe me a sit-down talk. We didn't get far today."

"True, but at least you have the rest of the body now, so you have the identity of the dead woman. That's a good start. The husband must know something. Anyway, I'm going to shove off so you can get busy. You have lots of work to do, that's for sure." Jess put out her hand. "I wish you luck. Call me when you're ready, and we'll finish that interrupted lunch some other time, my treat."

Beth reached to shake her hand. "Thanks. We'll do that. And you be sure to call me if you hear something I should know."

"Deal."

As Jess walked back to her truck, she couldn't help wondering what good-ol'-boy Butch was going to have to say about his now-dead wife when Beth interviewed him. Every tidbit of gossip she'd heard was that they barely tolerated each other and fought constantly about anything and everything. That raised the question of why they hadn't gotten a divorce a long while ago. There must've been some compelling reason, like maybe she had all the money or the sex was amazing, but for the life of her she couldn't figure it out.

Chapter Seven

JESS LIVED IN WHAT was billed as an RV "resort." It said so on the front sign. Most of the people who lived there during the winter were snowbirds who brought down their pricey Class-A motorhomes and fifth wheel recreation vehicles and stayed in them for the season. There were a few people in the park that lived there year-round, either in their RV or in manufactured houses called park models that were small enough to fit on an RV lot. There were only a few of those park models in the resort and Jess owned one of them. She'd bought hers new and then added onto it, putting on an extra room and a nice-sized covered porch. She loved it. With no carpet and not much to clean or decorate, it was exactly enough for her.

Sunday afternoon, she sat on her porch with her bare feet propped up on her wicker coffee table. Her left hand held a Bacardi and Pepsi. The other hand was thumbing through emails on her phone. She loved that part of each day, especially in the fall. The weather was warm but no longer as humid and hot as summer. Huge oaks shaded the streets, and the park's snowbirds had just started arriving.

As she looked up absently from her phone, she saw a brown speckled gecko run across her porch rail. It stopped, bounced up and down a few times, then inflated and deflated its bright red throat pouch as it looked around for another of its kind.

She shook her head and laughed. "Good luck, buddy."

Jess hadn't thought a whole lot about the incident out at Leisure Lakes and, quite frankly, intended to stay out of the whole thing. However, she knew it was her duty to give Beth any help she could if it didn't involve any real police-type work. She was done with all that. She simply wanted to live a nice, quiet life working in enough yards to keep her hands and mind busy and enjoy her retirement. She'd earned it.

She took another sip from her sweating glass before setting it on the table beside her. She laid her phone on the loveseat cushion next to her and relaxed her head back against the side of the house. Closing her eyes, she took a deep breath, letting it out in a soft sigh. This is the life she always thought about having after retirement. No responsibilities other than to her customers and no entanglements to complicate her life. She didn't see herself getting involved with another woman in a romantic way either. Nope, done with that, too. That didn't mean she couldn't enjoy friendship and an occasional date, but after two failed long-term relationships and several failed short-term ones, she figured she'd served her stint. No more.

Apparently falling in love was the kiss of death to every relationship she'd had. She knew it could've had something to do with her hard-driving work ethic—first as a uniformed officer and then as a detective. Working long hours and way too many nights took its toll on her body and mind, making it hard for her to have anything left for a partner. She knew it was partly the job, but it was also partly her fault. It was what it was. Even dating another cop didn't work. Too much stress on both ends and conflicting schedules doomed that one from the start. That, she figured, was the last try.

She believed she was fine alone now, keeping regular hours and working for herself. If it rained, she could stay home and work another day. She hadn't even gotten a dog because she wasn't sure she wanted the bother of taking care of it.

Maybe I should get a cat, she thought. *From what I've seen, cats don't need a lot of care. They're independent and all they require are food, water, and a clean litter box.* A sudden image of herself broke in that wasn't pretty. *Oh Lord, I could become one of those cat ladies I see out at Leisure Lakes who have several cats to keep them company. Nope. No way. No cat.*

Her phone went off, one of those nondescript ringtones that came with it. Still chuckling to herself about the cat lady thing, she sat back up to reach for the phone. She didn't even look at the caller ID. "Hello."

"Hi, is this Jess? It's Beth."

"Oh, hi." She sat straight up and put her feet down on the wooden planks of the porch. "Yes, it's me. What's up?"

"Did I interrupt anything? I hope you weren't busy."

"No, no. I was just sitting out here on my porch, talking myself out of getting a cat."

"You were...what?"

"Nothing. I wasn't doing anything. Well, there is a rum and Pepsi in front of me, so I guess I'm doing something."

"That sounds good. Got an extra one? I wasn't doing anything and thought I'd see what you were up to."

"I'm sure there's enough for a few more, actually. Come on over. You'll find my address on the back of my card. If you let me know when you're almost here, I'll meet you at the gate and let you in."

"Works for me. So, you don't trust me with your gate code, huh?" She could hear Beth laughing.

Jess smiled to herself, letting out a little chuckle. "Nope, I don't think we're good enough friends for that yet. Hang around long enough, though, and you could qualify."

Beth was still laughing. "I see. I'm driving a red Chevy Equinox. I'll be there in a few."

Jess decided she'd better put Beth in her contacts for future reference.

Chapter Eight

JESS DIDN'T BELIEVE IN making a mess if she could avoid it, and when she couldn't avoid it, she cleaned it up as soon as she finished. Being a bit of a neatnik did have its pluses—for one, she didn't need to run around doing a quick clean up when someone came to visit. Today was no exception. "Yard shoes" sat by each of the doors into the house that she put on whenever she left the porch. Her work boots sat on a rack near the door as well. She usually went barefoot or in socks because it kept the house cleaner. Besides, barefoot was much more comfortable than wearing shoes.

When Beth's call came that she was a few minutes away, Jess reached inside the front door for the golf cart keys that hung on a hook there and then slipped on a pair of flip flops before heading down the front porch steps for the golf cart. She made it to the park gate a couple of minutes before she saw Beth's SUV coming in the RV park entrance. She waved at Beth and hit the button on her remote to open the front gate. As Beth came through, Jess motioned for her to follow.

As she led Beth down one street and turned onto a couple more, Jess wondered what Beth was thinking about the RV park. Most of the park's lots still sat empty, with the concrete pads and small storage sheds awaiting the return of their snowbird residents. The ones who had returned already had their little yard ornaments and name plaques carefully reinstalled. When they reached Jess' site, she motioned for Beth to pull into her driveway as Jess parked her golf cart on a neighbor's empty site.

Jess left her golf cart and cut across her own front lawn, getting back to her driveway as Beth got out of her car. "Hi there! I'm kind of surprised to see you driving a smallish SUV on your day off. When I saw it the other day, I thought it was your work car. I figured your own would be something bigger, considering you used to drive in snow and the like up north."

"Oh, I did have something bigger, a Ford Expedition. It always got me where I needed to go in any kind of weather. Right after I moved to Florida, I got this pretty little thing." Beth patted its hood. "Boy, does it save me on gas and insurance. I love it." Beth waved her arm at Jess' house and small yard. "You have a cute place here. I don't think I've ever seen anything like this. Is it a trailer or what?"

"It's called a park model. It's a manufactured house made small enough to fit on an RV lot. I'll show it to you if you like."

"I'd love to see it. Does something cold come with the tour?"

Jess grinned. "I'm sure I can arrange that." She led the way up the steps to the porch, slipped off her flip flops at the door, and held the door open for Beth.

"Would you rather I took my shoes off, too?"

"You can if you like. It's up to you. I just happen to like being barefoot."

"Barefoot sounds good to me. I'm trying to get used to living here, and I've come to like the 'no shoes' thing a lot of people here seem to enjoy." Beth slipped off her sandals by the door and stepped inside, with Jess following close behind.

"One thing you learn right away down here is to make sure you don't leave your door open more than a few seconds, unless you don't mind flies, frogs, or geckos in your house. Worse, you could let in the mosquitos in summer. Some friendly, free advice."

"Thanks, I'll remember that." Beth looked around the room. "This room is cute. What is it?"

"I call it my office. I use my desk there for keeping track of my business. Ah, you noticed the bookcases." Beth nodded. "I'm a big fan of James Patterson and Sue Grafton, among others. I lend my books out to friends and they get passed around this place and returned to me later."

"Actually, I was looking at all those awards and trophies between your books."

"Um...well, I didn't want to leave them in a box, so I put them to work holding up the books. I played a lot of softball while I was still working. It was a great stress release."

"Yes, those are nice. To tell you the truth, I was admiring some of those other ones." Beth pointed to one of the awards. "What about all the ones with the badges on them?"

"Oh, those. I was just doing my job. Anyway, want to see the rest of the house? This room is the addition." She ignored the questioning look on Beth's face and her shoulder shrug and led the way through an archway. "This used to be the entry from the outside. Now it's a little hallway with a stacked washer and dryer here behind folding doors." She indicated the open door opposite. "And here's the bathroom." They took a few steps forward to a 'T' which formed the galley kitchen. "If you stand in one place here in the kitchen with your back to the sink, you can see every room in the house."

Jess watched as Beth stood where she indicated and looked in all directions. She watched her taking in the bedroom, with built-in dressers on one side, a closet on the other, and a window on the back wall. There was enough room to walk around the blue and white quilt-covered bed which sat under the window, but not much more. Looking the other way, there was a small, bright, and airy living room with Old Florida-looking painted white wicker furniture.

Jess assumed Beth was thinking the house was awfully small when she didn't say anything. "Come on into the living room. Oh, and here to your left is my dining area." She indicated a small round counter-height table with two tall chairs. "I like to look out the window while I'm eating."

"You know, this layout is quite clever. Everything's built in and tidy. I noticed the bedroom and bathroom doors are pocket doors, which saves space. What really opens the space up is the straight shot from the front to the back. Nothing to break it up and make it look cramped. Nice."

"I'm happy here. The large windows are what I like best. It lives bigger than it looks like it would from the outside, especially with that bay window across the front. The sliding glass doors going out to the porch from the living room help, too. Are you ready for that rum and Pepsi now? We can sit outside if you'd like."

"Sure, that'd be great. I do like your house. It looks like what I thought you'd live in, except a little smaller. Still, it seems to fit you. No pets?"

"Thanks. And no, no pets." Jess reached into an upper cabinet for another glass and into another cabinet for the Bacardi bottle. "I've never had time to care for a dog or cat, or even a goldfish for that matter. When I was on the job, I was too busy and worked odd hours. Now I don't have the inclination. I guess I've gotten used to living alone. I like not having to take care of someone or something else other than myself, my truck, and the house here."

Beth laughed. "So that was what you meant when you said you were talking yourself out of getting a cat. Very funny."

Jess chuckled as she turned to the refrigerator and retrieved two cans of Pepsi. "I have that conversation with myself occasionally. My friends here at the park keep telling me I shouldn't be alone and that I should think about getting a pet. Cat. Dog. Goldfish. Turtle. Whatever. I do briefly think about it now and again, like today, and each time I decide the answer is still a definite no."

Beth leaned her back against the kitchen counter and watched Jess pouring the soda into the glasses, refilling her own and filling a new one for Beth. "Yeah, me neither. I've never been able to make time for housetraining a dog. I hate having to worry about being home to give it some quality time. I've always thought pets are like kids. If you're not going to spend time with them, what's the point of having them?"

"That's exactly how I look at it. What's the point? The pet would have no quality of life other than a roof over its head, along with regular food and water." She seemed to regard the glasses for a second, poured in some of the clear rum, and mixed them with a teaspoon she retrieved from a drawer. "That seems mean to the animal and excessive worry for the pet parent, as they call them now." She held one glass up for Beth. "Want to taste this? I can put in a little more soda or rum, depending on how you like it."

Beth took a sip. "Perfect. Just needs a little ice."

"Ah, I knew I was forgetting something."

Chapter Nine

A COUPLE OF MINUTES later, Beth settled into the cushions of one of the dark brown wicker porch chairs and Jess returned to the settee. They raised their glasses to, "Cheers," and took a sip. Jess set her glass down and put her feet back up on the coffee table. She invited Beth to do the same, which she did. Jess tried to ignore Beth's cute toes with sunset pink nail polish on them, which were inches away from her own, but it was hard. She made a point of picking up her drink and swishing the ice cubes around again before taking a sip and setting it back down.

Beth took a sip of her rum and Pepsi before letting out a small sigh as she sank into the cushions. "Yep, this is the life. So, you like being retired?"

Jess smiled. "I do. Retirement definitely is all it's cracked up to be. I stay as busy as I care to, and I stay out of police business."

Beth raised her eyebrows. "You're sure you don't miss it at all?"

She shook her head. "I'm sure. I don't miss the long hours, the stake-outs, being shot at, or any other stuff of that sort."

"When you put it like that, no, I guess not. Don't you miss figuring out the 'who did it' part, or trying to prove who did it when you're sure who it was?"

Jess regarded her. "Maybe a little. For that, there are books to read or mysteries to watch. It's much safer. No one shoots at you and you're not chasing bad guys through alleys full of trash or worse. Oh, and another thing, you're not up all night trying to figure it out because a family is waiting for answers."

"Hmm...I suppose you have a point. I don't think I'm quite there yet. Fortunately, the uniformed officers or the younger detectives chase down most of the criminals while I get to try to figure it out. I do like that part, providing closure and justice. Even with all that said I know the time's coming in a few years. Right now, retirement is one of those things that I look at and admire in other people."

"That's good, then. It means you still enjoy your job. Besides, you haven't been here long. Although it's a similar job to what you did in upstate New York, it's different because it's here in Florida, right? For instance, you never had a dead body left for gator bait up there?"

"Uh, no..." Beth grinned. "Shortage of alligators. Up there we've had bodies mauled by black bears or frozen under snow. You probably didn't see much of that here."

"Not really. Shortage of snow in particular. Speaking of alligators...is there any news on whether an alligator killed 'what's her name' over there at Leisure Lakes? Or was it more likely the human killer variety, or an accident?"

"The only thing we know for sure is that the leg was bitten off, most likely by an alligator. Other than that, the jury is still out. The ME is just now getting to Rita. It seems they've been quite busy over there. Have you heard anything more from your gossiping customers?"

"Oh, it's still the usual stuff going around, although some of them think an alligator actually ate part of her." Jess shook her head slowly. "You wouldn't believe how some of these stories have evolved into fantastic tales so crazy they sound like science fiction."

Beth rolled her eyes. "I can imagine. That's gossip for you."

A man on a bicycle rolled by and waved. "Hey, Jess!"

"Hey, Chris!" she yelled back as she waved. To Beth she said, "I used to live down the street and next door to him when I first came here. I rented a place until I was sure I wanted to live in an RV resort instead of an apartment or house. Nice guy. By the way, some of the Leisure Lakes residents are ready to take up a petition to keep George from being 'arrested' and taken away. Is there any progress on that front?"

"They haven't ruled out that prospect, but so far they haven't sworn out a warrant for him or any of the other resident alligators." Beth started to giggle. "Can you imagine the handcuffs they'd have to put on an alligator? And how would they get past those jaws to put them on!" She broke out in laughter, with Jess joining in.

"They definitely couldn't handcuff his hands behind him without at least five sets of cuffs, that's for sure. And how could you march him out of the lake, anyway? Two scuba divers?" That mental picture of scuba divers with flapping flippers, holding the gator upright between them by each of its "arms" made them both laugh so hard they had tears overflowing onto their cheeks.

Jess couldn't help adding in, trying to talk as she laughed and mopped her eyes with her t-shirt. "Then they'd have to get him into the back of the squad car. First, they'd have to wrangle him in, with that tail of his swishing back and forth trying to get them. Do you suppose they could even seatbelt him in?"

A couple of minutes later, they caught their breaths and wiped their eyes. Jess shook her head. "Wow! I haven't laughed that hard in a long time. Unfortunately, we were having a laugh at poor George's expense. I don't think he'll mind, at least not yet."

Beth took a sip from her glass. "I haven't either. That was hilarious. I do hope we won't need to haul your George away, but if it looks like he did it, well...I'd hate to have to, but we would."

"I know. If he did kill her, some people would love to pat him on the back for getting rid of her. Now that Rita's dead, you can bet there's a lot more dirt going around about her." Jess swirled the ice cubes in her drink. "I'm sure I'll hear about that on Monday, and if it's anything at all, I'll let you know."

"Thanks. I'm sure you will. In the meantime, I understand Jim—or Butch, as I think he calls himself—didn't get along with his wife. Do you have any idea how bad it was?"

"I don't do their yard, so I don't have anything to do with them, personally. I do take care of the Blake's yard, and Kathy Blake was one of Rita's inner circle. Fortunately for me, Kathy's one of my few female customers who don't come out to talk my ear off while I'm there. I've only seen the husband on a few occasions, and even then just in passing, but he always smiles and waves at me. I almost never see her because they pay me through a bill-pay service."

"Why is that fortunate?"

"Because I hear she can be a real witch. A friend of hers, Sharon Zaxby, is also one of my customers, and Kathy sometimes tells Sharon gossip. Sharon isn't part of Rita's little group, but she loves hearing stories about Rita. I also think Kathy likes being able to tell that gossip to someone outside of the group. Maybe it makes her feel superior. Sharon doesn't care, from what I can see, and sometimes she tells me what Kathy told her—even if I don't want to hear it."

Beth leaned forward. "Like what?"

"Oh, like how much Rita liked to flirt with the guy that lives next door to them. I don't know if he liked it or not. It's a good bet the guy's wife didn't."

Jess could see Beth's mental notebook take that down for future reference. "You'd likely win that bet. So, do you think the wife could've had it in for her?"

"Anything's possible. I've never met her, so I have no idea if she's the type to do anything about it other than seethe or yell at her hubby. The women outnumber the men in this place about five to one, at least from what I've seen. I imagine if Rita flirted with him, she did it with lots of others, and that couldn't have gone over in a good way."

"No, I can imagine not. I've seen pictures of her at the clubhouse functions and they showed her dressed rather provocatively. When I interviewed her husband at their house, however, the pictures they displayed of themselves showed her wearing more conservative outfits. That makes me wonder if that was because her husband didn't like her dressing like that."

Jess mulled it over for a few seconds. "Good question. That's always possible. It could be part of their disagreements, along with whether he caught her flirting. I heard she was pretty obvious about it, but who knows if he caught her doing it." Jess took a sip from her glass. "I also heard that if someone called her on it, she'd laugh and say something about how she was only fooling around and that she wouldn't have that particular man on a stick."

Beth laughed. "On a stick, huh? I don't think I've heard that one before, although I think I get the gist of it just the same."

Jess grinned. "Anyway, like I said, that was entirely hearsay—and third or fourth hand, at that. I've never even met Rita in person, let alone seen her in action. I've seen her riding around in her golf cart or walking across the parking lot at the clubhouse with her gaggle of cronies. That's pretty much it."

Beth giggled. "Her gaggle, huh? They reminded you of geese. All right then, do you know who was in that group besides Kathy? I can interview them to see if they know anything that might shed some light on this."

"I only know them by sight, not by name. Butch probably knows who they are, or Kathy might."

"According to Rita's husband, no one disliked her enough to kill her. He said she seemed to be friends with quite a few people in the area. He also said she belonged to several community groups, although he wasn't sure which ones. She went to meetings or gatherings several times a week, usually during the day while he was at work. When I asked him if she had a calendar or schedule, though, he said he'd never seen one."

Jess shook her head slowly. "Look, I don't know about you, but I keep a calendar on the wall and on my computer. I can also access the computer one on my phone." She laughed. "Quite frankly, if it's not on the calendar, it doesn't happen."

Beth grinned. "Getting old and forgetful, are you?"

"Fifty-nine is hardly old." Jess laughed. "It has more to do with being retired. On the days I'm not doing yards the days just run into each other, which is fine with me. We do have activities here at the RV resort, most of them during snowbird season. If I want to remember to go to a potluck or anything else, I need to put it on the calendar. Same with doctor appointments or the like. As I said, if it's not on the calendar, it doesn't happen in my world. The point I'm trying to make is that Rita must've kept a calendar if she was that busy. She had to keep it on her phone or on one of those little paper booklets. You know, the ones they sell in drugstores with the pictures on the front."

"So far, her phone hasn't turned up, and I don't think they've dumped her handbag yet. As a matter of fact, I didn't see one at their house that contained anything. It's possible she wasn't carrying one."

"Always possible I guess, but she had to have a phone. Everyone does around here. I'll bet she had the latest whatever the trendy thing is now. Since she was wearing those neon pink running shoes when someone did her in, she might've been into other stylish stuff like that. I assume someone did her in since you haven't mentioned this was looking like an accident."

"No, we haven't made that call yet. Somehow, it doesn't feel like an accident. I mean, anything's possible, but I don't get the gut feeling it was."

"She had plenty of enemies there. For someone to hate her enough to kill her, well, that's another matter altogether. What I'm getting at is that Rita's probably acted like that for years now, and no one has bothered to even take a swing at her as far as I know, let alone kill her. I've never heard of anyone saying anything much back to her, to her face. That doesn't mean it didn't happen. What it does mean is that it didn't make enough of the rumor circuit to land on my ears. To tell you the truth, that hasn't bothered me at all. I get tired of hearing who did what to whom or who's sleeping with whom."

Beth's eyes got big. "What?"

Jess laughed. "Oh, yes, that kind of thing still goes on even among the eighty-year-olds, believe me."

Beth shook her head and made an 'I don't believe it' face. "Seriously? I guess I didn't think about that. My mom's in her eighties, and I just can't imagine...or maybe I don't want to."

Jess laughed again as she reached for her glass. "Yeah, it happens. At least it does out there, from what I've heard. In fact, there's a retirement community somewhere here in Florida—a quite upscale one—that holds a record for venereal disease cases."

Beth blinked hard and shook her head again. "No. Really? You're messing with me now, aren't you?"

"Nope. Remember, it's what I've heard. It's possible you could research something like that online, but I've never tried. What kind of search parameter would you put in? I also heard that they hand out penicillin like candy there."

"Wow. I've never imagine anything like that."

"That's what's going around, anyway. Then again..." Jess shrugged. "It's unsubstantiated. The stories that come out of that place blow you away, though. I wouldn't live there on a bet, even though people like me rarely get an STD."

"What do you mean, people like you?"

Jess grinned. "I only like women. Or didn't you figure that out already? Most people do, they just don't say anything about it."

"I'll admit it crossed my mind, but since it didn't have anything to do with anything, it didn't matter."

Jess smiled bigger. "I guess that's a good thing then."

Beth picked up her drink again. "It's not like I'm out looking for a girlfriend of that kind. I haven't had any kind of female friend in ages. Seems like working and socializing with groups of cops, most of them men, kind of keeps me out of that."

Jess held up her drink. "Yeah, I get that. Plus, after the end of a shift, you're too tired to hang out anywhere other women congregate, right?"

"That's about it. I've been hanging around the guys so long, I'm not even sure how I'd act on an actual date." Beth sat back in her chair. "Anyway, that's neither here nor there. No one's going to ask me out any time soon. Being a cop and a detective on top of that kind of puts people off."

"I've felt that way, too. Once they find out what you do, they don't want to go out with you again. But you know what? The single life isn't that bad, now, is it? You can come and go as you please, right?"

Beth held up her drink in salute. "Right. On the other hand, you don't have anyone waiting for you to come home at night."

"I see that as a plus. There's no one waiting for you, so you can stop on the way home and have dinner, meet a friend for a drink, or even run into a store without consulting someone else. You can go the drive through route and get something or fix whatever you want for supper without asking her what she wants. Worse yet, you don't come home starving, to whatever she made and find it's something you don't like."

"Wow. You've given this a lot of thought."

Jess shook her head slowly. "No, just been there and done that. I guess I've been through enough relationship stuff to know what I don't want."

"Sounds like it. So, would you ever consider another relationship or are you completely done with all of that?"

Jess pursed her lips and tilted her head as she considered. "My gut response is that I'm done with that whole thing. On second thought, my answer is that I'm not looking, but if the perfect woman fell into my lap, I guess I'd consider it." She laughed, looking away as she reached for her rum and Pepsi and swirled the ice cubes in it before taking a swallow. "How's that for a reply?"

"That's what I kind of figured you'd say. I suppose you'd have to reconsider if the perfect partner dropped out of the sky. 'Reconsider' is the operative word, right? At least you're keeping an open mind about it. That's a good attitude for a former detective." Beth laughed as she winked at her. "You need to keep an open mind to make sure you don't miss any clues."

Chapter Ten

MONDAY MORNING FOUND JESS back at work at Leisure Lakes. It was her regular day to work at Sharon Z's house, and as usual, Sharon came out there with her coffee cup to regale Jess with the latest news. Most of the time, Jess listened with one ear and let it go out the other. Today she found herself paying a little more attention in case Sharon said something worth listening to.

Sharon was droning on with one of her stories while Jess clipped the morning glory vines on the carport trellis. "So anyway, I heard that Rita put on quite a display at last weekend's potluck at the clubhouse."

Jess stopped and looked at her. "The weekend before this last one?"

Sharon nodded before she took another sip from her coffee.

"What kind of display?"

"I wasn't at that one because I had one of my migraines. I heard, though, that Rita verbally beat up a woman from the other side of this place. She was some poor little defenseless eighty-something. I think her name was Edith. Rita even made her cry." Her eyes squinted. "That's pretty low. I mean, really, the woman didn't even know Rita from what I heard. Rita decided to pick on her for the way she dressed or some other stupid thing. Everyone there heard it."

Jess stopped her clipping. "Wow. That's awful, all right. I wonder why she'd stoop so low to do such a thing. And no one stopped her?"

"From what I've heard, Rita never needed an excuse. And no, no one stopped her until Butch grabbed her. I think the other residents were glad it wasn't them. Rita always did whatever she felt like, even flirting with other guys at these things. When I saw her do it, it always looked like she was trying to get a rise out of the wife or girlfriend."

Jess sighed. "I heard the same thing about her from someone else. She sure was a real piece of work. I'm surprised Butch stayed married to her."

"Me, too. I once asked Kathy why they stayed married and she shrugged it off saying she had no idea. I've always thought maybe Rita was the one with the money between them. I doubt it could've been the sex since I heard they'd stopped sleeping in the same bedroom."

"You sure hear a lot. To be honest, though, that doesn't sound like something a person would brag about. I can't imagine Rita would've told that to anyone."

"Oh, you'd be surprised at the things Rita told her buddies." Sharon stepped a bit closer and lowered her voice. "Just between you and me, that last thing about separate bedrooms was something Rita did tell Kathy and the others. She told them in that last week or so before she died that she was done putting up with his idea of sex, which was more like jumping on her and getting it over with."

Jess grimaced. "I guess that wouldn't be so great, would it?"

"Not at all." Sharon pointed her finger and waggled it at Jess. "Now, don't you tell anyone I told you all that stuff. Kathy told me everything in strict confidence because she was told not to tell anyone. Of course, Kathy could tell me because she knew she could trust me to keep it private."

"I'm sure she did." Jess mentally rolled her eyes, wondering how many others Sharon had told. She tried to maintain her sympathetic facial expression. "It's obvious that Kathy sees you as a good friend."

Sharon stood up a little straighter. "Oh, I am. I'm always here for her to unload on. To tell you the truth, I don't think she cares for Rita as much as she used to. I assume she just puts up with her because they've known each other so long. She said Rita needed friends but didn't have that many."

"I can sort of see why, if she acted like that."

"Apparently, she didn't say nasty things to her actual friends. Rita seemed to be quite loyal to them, or at least they were quite loyal to her. I do know that Rita and Kathy go back a long way. They knew each other way before they moved into Leisure Lakes."

Jess felt her ears prick up at that. "Really? That's fascinating."

"Rita was Kathy's oldest friend, truth be told. Rita and her first husband, Carl, were close with Kathy and her first husband, Jack. I can't remember what the connection was. They could've been neighbors, or the husbands may have worked together. Maybe Rita and Kathy did. I can't remember the particulars. Anyway, they were quite tight as a group. Rita and Kathy lost their husbands within about a year of each other and they both later remarried. Kathy and Ed moved away, and Rita and Kathy lost touch. Kathy and Ed bought into Leisure Lakes right after it opened. Years later, she said they ran into each other again here after Rita and Butch moved in, when Butch took over as the manager."

"That must've been quite a surprise."

"Oh, yes. Kathy said both she and Rita were happy and surprised to find each other here. She told me she was glad to reconnect with her old friend, even though their new husbands have never become close."

"That explains why at least one of those women hangs around with Rita, I guess."

"I guess so. Well, I'd better go in, since I've got a grocery run to do. See you in a couple of weeks, Jess. Your check will be in the usual place."

"Thanks. See you then."

Jess finished up Sharon's yard using her leaf blower to clear the driveway and along the street after she'd edged them. Her mind kept running over what she'd heard, thinking maybe Butch did have a reason to get rid of Rita. It was conceivable that he could've had enough after he was relegated to the other bedroom with no sex anymore. He did look genuinely surprised, though, when they lifted the tarp on the body. Was he shocked she was dead, or was he just surprised they even found her body? Anyway, Jess decided, it was something Beth should know, and sooner rather than later.

Back in her truck, Jess texted Beth to let her know she had some information for her that might be useful. She asked her to call when she was available. Beth must've been busy because it was over an hour before a return text came that she was at the clubhouse again. She said she was just looking around and to come on over. Jess had finished her last yard, ready to head home anyway.

It only took a few minutes to drive over to the clubhouse and then look around the outside to find Beth. She was standing on the fishing pier that extended into the lake and she appeared to be examining the pier pilings. Jess called her name as she approached to get her attention.

Beth turned around and stuck her hand up in a wave as Jess came down the pier. "Hi, Jess. What's up?"

Jess leaned against one of the pier posts, making sure she didn't get too close to Beth. She was still quite dirty, even after brushing herself off. "I heard something interesting about Rita and Butch today on the gossip circuit. Thought you might like to hear it."

"Of course I want to hear it." Beth leaned a little bit closer. "All right, give."

"Sometime in the last week or so before she died, Rita told her little circle that she had kicked Butch out of their bedroom and he was sleeping in the guest room. The stated reason was that lately his idea of sex was one of those slam-bam-thank-you-ma'am things."

Beth looked puzzled.

"Jump on and jump off?"

Apparently, a light bulb went on as Beth said, "Ah, I got it. No foreplay, just get his jollies."

"Right. At first, I was surprised she told that to anyone. On second thought, that does sound like something that a woman would say who likes to flaunt her dominance. I bet Butch wasn't telling his buddies about it."

Beth shrugged. "You never know. It's odd the things people tell other people. I mean, I wouldn't tell anyone if I'd been kicked out of my spouse's bedroom, but I've stopped being surprised by what other people tell about their private lives."

Jess made a face, raising her eyebrows. "I'd be so embarrassed if my girlfriend told people I was an awful lover."

Beth chuckled. "Me too. I'm guessing that's never happened to you, right?"

Jess shook her head and grinned. "Nope, it hasn't. I've been accused of many things, but being a bad lover—no. Anyway, if Rita had cut him off, it couldn't have made him happy. It did make me wonder who had the money in the family. I'm betting on her or he'd have left her long ago with her acting like she did. Now that she's dead, maybe he gets everything. Anyway, goes to motive. I thought you might find the information helpful."

"Thanks for the info. It's something to investigate. We're interviewing her 'gaggle of cronies,' as you called them. I wonder if any of them will speak ill of her now. Lots of people won't say bad things about someone after they're dead, but sometimes they're willing to spill their guts with all kinds of stories they've held back. You never can tell."

Jess pushed away from the piling but turned and rested her arm on it. "At any rate, I thought you'd want to know. Oh, and I heard one other thing that may or may not be useful. Kathy Blake and Rita knew each other long before they came here. They were each married before and the couples were close. The husbands died, the ladies remarried, and according to what I heard, they lost touch for quite a few years until Butch and Rita moved here. Although the women rekindled their friendship, the new husbands don't have much to do with each other. They probably have nothing in common. All of that may have nothing to do with anything, but..."

"It's hard to figure out where something will lead. In most cases, it's the husband or wife who has the most reason to do away with them."

"True. Anyway, if I hear anything else, you'll be the first one I call. Are you making any progress? Assuming she was murdered, do you have any idea where it happened?"

"The working theory is that she was killed here since they found her body, or at least most of it, in this lake. The crime scene people checked the pier and didn't find anything, but it has rained quite a bit since it happened. She appeared to have been in the water a few days, and people hang around out here on the pier and the shore a lot, so there shouldn't be much of anything to find. I'm doing a lot of thinking and walking around looking at stuff, anyway."

Jess grinned at her. "Stuff, huh? It's a great technical term and I used it often. So, have you seen George yet? He likes to hang out near this lake. You'll know it's him because he has a scar on the top of his nose."

"Really. The top of his nose?"

"I heard he got it trying to reach a bird on the other side of a chain link fence and scraped it up good."

"Nope, no George so far. Could he have heard we were after him and he's lying low now?" Beth smiled.

Jess stared at her. "Really? You're looking for him?"

"No, I'm just giving you a hard time. We still haven't figured out how she died for sure."

"Let me know if you need someone to bounce things off. I'm a good listener."

"And I'm always up for another rum and coke...or lunch, if you like. I enjoy talking with you."

"You, too. You've got my number."

Beth grinned. "Yes, I think I do."

Chapter Eleven

"I'VE GOT SOME NEW ideas I'd like to run by you. How would you like to come to my house for dinner tonight? I promise I can cook." Beth had launched right into it when Jess answered her phone. It had only been a few hours since she'd seen her on the pier.

"Thanks for the invitation. I'd love to. I'm always up for free food I don't need to cook, and I'm not a fussy eater. You sound rather excited. Does that mean you got the autopsy results back?"

"Yes, but there's more. Anyway, I can't talk about it right now. Can you come over at six-thirty? Or is that too late? I know some people around here eat earlier."

"No, that's fine. Wouldn't you rather meet in a restaurant, though, so you don't have to cook on a weeknight?"

"No, I'd rather have a little more privacy to talk. Besides, I like to cook, and I'd love to have company. You'll be my first guest at my Florida home."

"Well then, it will be my pleasure. What can I bring?"

"How about dessert? I'm making a roasted chicken, so something light would be great."

"I'll make that happen. I'm looking forward to hearing your news."

"I'll text you my address as soon as I hang up. See you at six-thirty, or you can come a little earlier if you like."

Jess smiled to herself as she dropped the phone into her cargo shorts pocket. Six-fifteen, then. She found herself wondering again about whether Beth was looking for more than friendship. Maybe it was nothing, and she knew it was silly to try to figure it out this early on. Anyway, she decided she wouldn't mind looking at those green eyes and that red hair across the table.

Upon further consideration, she realized Beth was the first person in quite a while, other than her sister, that she'd looked forward to spending an evening with. Could it have something to do with enjoying talking about a case? Perhaps she simply enjoyed hanging out with her. Attractive, a fun laugh, and a sharp mind to boot. There were far worse things than spending an evening with her.

A short while later, Jess found herself wandering the aisles at

Publix, wondering what to bring for dessert. *How hard could this be? Something light, something light*, she repeated to herself. The first thing that popped into her head was Jell-O. She laughed. No. She loved Jell-O because her grandmother made it for her when she visited as a child. Nana always had more than one flavor of Jell-O in the fridge every time. It's a treat, but no, that wouldn't do to bring to Beth's.

Her wanderings took her to the bakery department. Most of the stuff in there looked yummy to the max but not light. *Eclairs, no. Cake, no. Pie? Not hardly. Wait. A little box of tiny creampuffs. They're mostly air except for that little bit of filling inside. That qualifies as light. Well, light enough anyway.* She pondered it for another few seconds before reaching for a box of cream puffs from the bakery cooler. She headed for the checkout lines, pleased with herself.

Callie at the ten-items-or-less register grinned at her as she rung her up. "Oh, Jess, creampuffs! You gonna eat these for supper or munch on 'em while you watch TV tonight?" She put the box in a bag, making sure the contents wouldn't get jumbled when picked up.

"Looks like you know me way too well, Callie. I can tell I need to go through someone else's checkout line more often." Jess grinned back at her. "As a matter of fact, I've been invited to dinner and this is my contribution. Think these babies will get me in the door?"

Callie squinted her eyes at her as she laughed. "You mean, like a date? Should I be jealous?"

Jess kept up their usual banter. "Oh, come on. There's no one like you. She's just a friend."

Callie held up the bag and waggled her eyebrows. "Sweetie, all I can say is they would get you in my door any day. If they don't go over tonight, bring them on to my house."

Jess reached for the bag. "I'll keep that in mind. See ya."

Callie clung to part of the bag. "Wait! There's no one behind you and since you work out there, I wonder if you've heard anything about that Leisure Lakes thing. I heard that woman was murdered, then I heard they might call it an accident. Do you know what the story is?"

"Last I heard, they're still working on the case. The woman was found in the lake by the clubhouse there, missing part of her leg. The talk going around is that it was an opportunistic gator bite that might've taken the leg, but who knows. I'm sure they'll figure it all out soon. I'll tell you one thing, though, the rumor mill is crazy busy."

"Don't you just know it! We get a lot of Leisure Lakes people shopping here, and believe me, they like to chat. If they're not talking to the checkers, they're gossiping to each other in line or to the baggers as they unload the carts outside."

Jess shook her head slowly. "That figures."

"Anyway, you being a former detective and all, I thought you might've heard or seen something worth knowing."

"Not really. Have you?"

Callie leaned in even closer. "Well…the rumor I heard—and it's just rumor, of course—is that the dead lady murdered her first husband and was about to do in the second when she got done in herself. Isn't that a doozy?"

"Wow, that's quite a rumor. When did you hear that?"

"Only this morning, believe it or not. I was working one of the regular lines and had to send someone to get a price code for something. While we waited, the customer and the one behind her, who seemed to know each other well, were going on about it. Now, we don't hear something like that in a grocery line often, believe me."

"I guess not. Did you know either of the ladies?"

"I've seen them in here often enough that I know their faces but don't know them by name. They must do their big shopping elsewhere, because they always pay cash. They never buy staples, just stuff you'd run out of, like milk or ice cream."

"Interesting. I must say, that's one rumor I hadn't heard, and believe me, I've heard plenty since this whole thing started. The latest rumors were ridiculous things, like it was a mob hit or something."

"Pretty silly, for sure. Okay then, got a customer. Anyway, great talking to you." Callie winked at Jess. "You have a nice evening."

Chapter Twelve

BETH'S THIRD FLOOR APARTMENT was in a large downtown complex intended for up and coming professionals. The four-story buildings were designed as ultramodern boxes, painted in various shades of grey with shots of coral in the graphics applied to them. When they first opened, Jess wondered what those apartments looked like. Out of curiosity, she almost went in to look once, but "almost" was as close as she'd come to checking it out. She had no intention of moving from her little house. She realized she was finally going to get a look at the mystery place. At exactly six-fifteen, Jess reached Beth's apartment. She shifted from one foot to the other a couple of times before tapping the bell button next to the door.

Beth greeted her in navy shorts and a red t-shirt. Her hair was wound up in one of those clips that could be used to close a bag of potato chips just as easily. She smiled warmly, waving Jess in with a little bow. "Welcome to my humble abode. And welcome to whatever's in that bag there. Can I take it from you?"

Jess handed over the beige plastic bag. "Sure. It's miniature cream puffs. I hope they'll be light enough. Oh, and by the way, the checkout lady at Publix said that if you didn't like them, she'd take them off your hands." She laughed.

"Oh, no. I love cream puffs, and I can guarantee you none of them will go to waste. May I get you something to drink? I have water, tea, Pepsi, or some wine or beer if you'd prefer."

"I'll have some Pepsi, please." Jess' head swiveled around to look at the apartment. "I've never been in this building before. With these light wood floors, it looks as modern inside as it does outside. It looks airy. How do you like it?"

"I like it now." Beth reached into the refrigerator for two sodas before putting the pastry box in. She opened one of the Pepsi bottles, handed it to Jess, and opened the other one for herself. "To tell you the truth, I wasn't sure about this place at first. What sold me is that the location's great and it's close enough to walk to all kinds of restaurants and to Manning Park for the farmers' market and stuff like that. I decided I could make it anything I wanted it to be. I happen to like clean, contemporary furniture, so my stuff fits in. Would you like a tour? Believe me, it won't take long. This place is pretty small."

"Thanks for the soda." Jess lifted the bottle in a salute and took a sip. "I'd love a tour. There's small and then there's tiny. Your place looks much bigger than mine."

"I'm sure it's not much bigger. I'd guess it's about two hundred square feet bigger than your place, including your porch in that estimate. When you came in through the dining and kitchen area, you got to see them. The kitchen is compact and works well enough for one person, but that's about it. The washer and dryer are right off the kitchen over there behind the double doors. We're standing in the living room, and if you look to your right, you can see my bedroom. Almost as fun as your place, standing in one spot to see the whole thing. There's a small balcony, as you can see, but it's so tiny I could barely put a chair on it, so I don't. I don't think it's meant for entertaining. I'm positive that balcony was only put on as a design element and a way to have sliding glass doors in the living room. They do bring in more light, and I think the screen will allow a breeze when it cools off."

Beth led the way through an open door into the bedroom. The bed showed off a teal green bedspread with white throw pillows. "Here's my bedroom. I'm quite fond of that big window. It also has a sizeable walk-in closet, but other than that, nothing to write home about. Big enough for me, at least. The bathroom's in there." She pointed around the corner. "It's actually roomier than I thought it would be, with a linen closet and all. Anyway, that's pretty much it. What do you think?"

"Your apartment feels airy. Doesn't feel tiny at all. Also, the teal bedspread is pretty," Jess said as she walked back into the living room and sat on the sofa. "I have to say it's much warmer looking in here than I envisioned when I saw the building. You've made a home for yourself, and that makes all the difference. Do you always keep vases of fresh flowers in your place?"

Beth smiled and sat in the club chair across from Jess. "Usually. I like flowers and pick them up weekly from the farmers' market. They make the place look more colorful. Since I don't have anyone in my life to buy me any, I buy them for myself whenever the mood strikes me, which is often. Do you think that's silly?"

Jess shook her head. "No, of course not. Why'd you think that? Who's going to take care of us if we don't take care of ourselves? As a matter of fact, I almost brought you a small bouquet or a plant as a sort of housewarming present, but I wasn't sure if you even liked flowers or plants. Some people hate flowers and are offended if you bring them what they call 'dead things.' I think they look pretty in here. You know, this place does look like you."

"Thanks. It's comfortable now that I've put everything away and made a final decision, for now, on the furniture arrangement. That blue couch has been on each of these walls. I've also arranged it facing the sliders, kind of like a room divider. I like that I can rearrange the furniture whenever I feel like it. At least here, there are options. My last place in New York was so tiny that there was only one way to fit anything in there."

"Oh, I've lived in places like that too, believe me. I'm glad I never had to live in a place like that for long."

A dinging sound came from the kitchen. "Ah, the chicken's ready. Hope you're hungry." Beth pushed herself up from her chair and, on her way to the kitchen, patted Jess on her bare thigh.

It was a light touch, and Jess told herself Beth meant nothing by it. That, however, didn't stop the little tingle it sent up her leg. *Good grief, has it been that long since someone who was not a relative touched me? Or is it just Beth?* She reached for the bottle of Pepsi on the side table and took a couple of sips from it. *Beth is probably one of those touchy-type people, and she does that to everyone without thinking about it.* Jess was going to assume that's what it was, anyway, and try to ignore her reaction to it. She was about to ask if she could set the table when she noticed it was already done. Washing her hands suddenly seemed like a great idea.

A couple of minutes later, Beth announced that dinner was ready. As soon as they were both seated, Beth silently bowed her head for a few seconds—Jess assumed it was for a short prayer—and then crossed herself.

Beth looked up afterward and smiled. "I'm Episcopalian. If I don't say a blessing before supper, my mom swears when she's gone, she'll rise up out of her grave and haunt me forever." She laughed. "At least that's what she has me believing, and I'm not taking any chances. I don't make it to worship services every Sunday because of work, but at least I can say a blessing at supper. Thanks for waiting for me; now go ahead and help yourself. I hope you like it."

"Thanks. Everything looks delicious. I was also raised Episcopalian, but I've gotten away from attending services. Too many Sundays on duty, I guess." Jess took a sliced piece of chicken breast and some mashed potatoes, and then poured gravy over them both. "Now this is a dinner. You don't always see gravy much nowadays, but I love it. And biscuits, too, nice."

"I'm going to guess you're not fond of green vegetables. Am I right?"

"You are. I stopped eating them when I stopped being forced to. I do seem to manage without them." She grinned sheepishly. "Once in a while I eat a few green beans. I just..."

Beth put her hand up. "Hey, that's fine. Everyone has their own thing. I'm not your mother." Beth laughed, and then raised her eyebrows. "Besides, you seem to be in good shape even without green veggies."

Jess felt herself blush just a tad. "Thanks. It's one of the reasons I stay busy working in people's yards. Keeps me from turning into a couch potato." She took a bite of her chicken and let out a little sigh. "Great chicken, with excellent gravy. My compliments to the chef."

"That's sweet of you. I'm glad you like it." Beth took a couple of bites from her dinner.

Jess had a thought. "By the way, you won't believe the rumor I heard today. This time it was at the grocery store, of all places. The checkout woman told me she heard two Leisure Lakes ladies chatting while standing in line. The latest rumor going around is that Rita did away with her last husband and was thinking about doing away with her current one. I wrote it off like the mobster hit rumors I heard until what you just said. Ain't that a kicker?"

Beth put her fork down and leaned on her elbows. "Wow. That's something, all right. It's amazing how rumors get around. We do know that Rita booted her husband out of her bedroom recently, so maybe it's not so crazy after all. I may have to check out that former husband's death."

Jess reached for a biscuit. "Butch couldn't have been happy about their bedroom situation. I mean, that would be humiliating big time, if she was telling her cronies about it and the story got circulated."

"Hmm...all I can say is there sure seems to be more to this situation than it looked like on the surface. There usually is, isn't there?"

"You got that. So, what did the autopsy report say?"

Beth picked up her fork and once again waved it in the air as she explained. "Ah, yes, the autopsy report. Her blood alcohol level was almost twice the DUI limit."

Jess stared at her. "Wow! That's bad."

"Well, from what I heard already from people, that's no surprise at all. However, the actual cause of death was drowning. She appears to have drowned after blunt force trauma to her head. They have confirmed an alligator bite took off that leg, but it was postmortem. There were also a couple more bite marks on her, like the same alligator was tasting her or another one came along for a taste, too. She also had multiple marks on her right arm that looked like someone had grabbed her hard. The main thing was that she didn't bleed to death from the leg amputation."

"So, someone bonked her over the head, and she was either pushed or fell into the lake and drowned?"

Beth took a small bite of her potatoes, then waved her fork around again as she spoke, punctuating her words by poking at the air. "Let's say she either hit her head or she was hit. Still open on that. Wood bits in the wound match the type of wood on the dock. That could also mean a fall, intentional or unintentional. I plan to question Butch again about what happened."

"Do you honestly think Butch killed his wife? He looked pretty upset when he saw her body."

"I don't know yet. He seems a logical suspect, but that doesn't mean anything solid. This whole thing could depend on a timeline we don't have yet. Either way, I'm fairly sure by now we can rule out the alligator as a murder suspect. It's looking like he or she was an opportunistic muncher."

"That's a relief."

"How come?"

"To tell you the truth, my sister was worried sick about animal control taking George away...or even worse, putting him down."

Beth set her fork down and stared at Jess, her brows furrowed. "Are you serious? If I hadn't heard it coming out of your mouth, I'd assume it was a joke. You don't look like you're kidding."

"I kid you not. I'm sure I mentioned that to you the first day we met. You were kind of busy, after all, so it's no surprise you don't remember. Anyway, most of the alligators out there have pet names once they get old enough to be recognizable as individuals. There are several that I see around on a regular basis. Let's see, there's Big Mack, Sam, and of course George, that I know of. I'm sure there are several more, but I can't come up with their names right now."

Beth started laughing. "Really? Big Mack? Come on..."

"It's true. He got his name because someone dropped a McDonald's container down by one of the lakes and he went after it.

The joke was that he must've been having a hamburger craving, so they started calling him Big Mack. He's not big at all yet, and I'm sure if he knew what they called him, he'd love it." Jess chuckled. "That's the story, anyway. Cute, huh?"

"Cute, yes." Beth shook her head. "Leisure Lakes is a much more fascinating place than one would think from looking at the surface."

"Oh, yeah. That place is full of stories, including who's doing what with or to whom, for instance. One string of conversation going around was about how long you should wait after someone dies to ask out the widow or widower. It's amazing how many of them marry one of their friends after their spouse dies. When I first came here, I was sure when one spouse died the other one moved back north to be near their kids...and some do. Most of them seem to stay here and find another partner, even if they don't remarry."

"I suppose that for some widows remarrying could cut off their income."

"That's what I hear. So, they 'live in sin'"—she put her fingers in the air like quotation marks—"or they maintain separate homes so their kids don't find out there's more going on than it appears."

"Fascinating. I'll file that away in the back of my head for future reference."

A few minutes later, Jess put her fork down on her empty plate. "That was an outstanding meal. My stomach thanks you for the excellent dinner, and the rest of me is happy to help with the dishes."

Beth grinned and patted Jess lightly on her arm. "It was my pleasure, and I'm glad you liked it. While I'll let you help clear the table, the dishes can wait. Are you interested in dessert right now, or would you prefer to wait a few minutes for some coffee to go with it? We can adjourn to the living room if you don't mind the wait."

Jess felt her cheeks warm a tiny bit at Beth's touch to her arm, but she managed to hide any other reaction with a laugh. "Oh...adjourning sounds quite upscale. I'd love to adjourn."

An hour later, coffee and cream puffs taken care of, they were saying good night on the way to Beth's door.

"Thank you for coming over as the first dinner guest at my new place. You've made me feel much more at home here. It's nice to have a friend to call for lunch or whatever. I mean, if you're good with that."

"I'm good with that. Thank you for having me over."

Beth threw her arms around Jess and hugged her before giving her a little kiss on the cheek, and then let her go before Jess could say anything else. Jess just smiled and said good night, then was out the door.

On the way to the car, Jess' warm face told her she was blushing. *Blushing? Really? At my age?* She rubbed at her cheeks to try to make it stop, even though it felt rather pleasant. *Okay, it's a very pleasant feeling,* she thought, even though the vibes she was trying to ignore hinted to her there could be more to this than a casual friendship. She wasn't sure she was ready for more than that.

Chapter Thirteen

THE NEXT MORNING, JESS was out in front of Mrs. Haverty's place, edging her driveway when Gabby Singleton stopped her golf cart to chat.

"Yoo hoo! Jess!" Gabby waved and yelled to be heard over the noise from Jess' equipment.

Jess turned off her edger, still holding it in her hand. Gabby would be mining her for gossip about the leg incident, but she had work to do. She was covered in yard debris and dirt, and Mrs. Haverty had already slowed her down by coming out to chat. Nevertheless, Jess smiled and waved back at her one of her favorite customers. "Hi, Gabby. What's up? Do you need something?"

"Oh, no. I'm fine. I thought I'd see if you've heard anything new about Rita's death. I saw you talking to that detective the other day out on the clubhouse pier."

"I happened by and saw her there. The police can't discuss the case with civilians, you know." Jess knew that last bit was a little lie, but Gabby didn't need to know that. There was a reason her nickname was Gabby, besides her first name being Gabriella.

Gabby didn't miss a beat. "I just saw that police detective going into the office again, too." She sat back in her seat with her arms crossed over her chest. "Do you have any idea what that's about?"

"I haven't a clue. You probably know more than I do."

"Well...I simply wondered if they were talking to Butch or interviewing the office staff. Anyway, since you don't know anything, I'll have to go see what's what after the detective leaves. Carol's always good for a chat when she's working the front desk. By the way, I thought you'd like to know that Edith seems to be doing much better now. To tell you the truth, I think she's rather enjoying all the attention she's getting."

Jess shook her head, shifting the edger to her other hand. "Don't you think she'd rather that leg had not landed in her backyard, Gabby? She's always been a quiet lady."

"Right. Well, maybe now. I heard she used to be a Las Vegas showgirl."

Jess had to put her edger down after that one. “Oh, come on. Edith? Seriously? Where does this stuff get started?”

“Who knows? If she was, she could be enjoying the attention.”

“If Edith was a dancer, it had to be many years ago. She’s nearly ninety years old. Besides, who cares if she was a performer when she was young? If so, I think it would be fascinating, not something to whisper about. It could be that the person who started that rumor is jealous that they haven’t done something interesting.”

“Are you suggesting that some people have had boring lives?”

Jess put her hand up. “Heck no! Besides, a fascinating life to one person might be boring to another. A librarian’s job, for instance, could be uneventful to some and quite the adventure to others. You can’t tell what someone has done earlier in their life by looking at them now, that’s for sure.”

“I can imagine.”

“All right, here’s an example for you. One time we arrested some sweet-looking grandfather. We had hardcore evidence he had murdered his first family forty years before. His neighbors were up in arms when we took him away in handcuffs. They were sure he couldn’t have done anything violent and we had the wrong man. One of the neighbors, an attorney, offered to defend him for free until he saw the evidence we had. It conclusively proved that mild-mannered old guy massacred his former family, including his wife, kids, and mother in law. Goes to show, you just never know.”

Gabby was staring by then. “Wow...you don’t, do you? I guess it’s true, especially in a place like this. I mean, we’ve all been places and done things that, on the surface, one would never guess. I mean, here you are, a retired police detective, doing yard work. Who would guess that?”

“I suppose no one would, but I imagine you had an interesting career of some kind before you retired, too.”

“Me? The only even slightly interesting thing I ever did was play softball. I was quite good at it, as a matter of fact. My batting average was the highest in the league for a while. Other than that, I’m not that interesting. I play golf now. I mean, after I married my Harold, God rest his soul"—Gabby crossed herself—“I’ve pretty much lived a quiet life. Before that, though, I’ll admit I was a bit of a rowdy.” She laughed. “That was many years ago and none of it included undressing on stage.”

“You played softball?” Jess asked, trying to change the subject. “That’s pretty cool. I’m sure that helped your golf game, didn’t it?”

"Actually, my instructor said the same thing. He mentioned that golf and softball share the same basic swing idea."

"You never know who you'll run into in this place, that's for sure. Anyway, it's been nice talking to you, Gabby. I'm sure you've got lots of things to do. I'll be over to do your yard soon." Jess reached down and picked up her edger but didn't start it.

"All right, I'll get going." Gabby turned away, and then looked back at Jess. "You know, you've got a good head on your shoulders." And with that, she was gone, leaving Jess wondering what that was all about as she pulled the starter cord.

Chapter Fourteen

BETH WAS BACK AT the Leisure Lakes office. As she waited to talk to Butch again, she wandered around the sales area, looking at the various layouts of the new homes for sale. In the middle of the room, a table held the typical subdivision map under glass. It showed the lakes and the homesites, with little colored pins showing which sites were sold and which ones under escrow. There were still quite a few empty homesites available. The manufactured houses for sale looked spacious and they were even in her price range, had she been looking for a new home.

She was toying with the idea of choosing one of the house plans for herself as something to pass the time, when Butch came out of his office. With him was a woman she assumed was a sales associate and a couple who looked like they were quite interested in buying a place. The saleswoman led the couple out the door toward one of the parked golf carts as Butch smiled widely and shook their hands.

His smile evaporated when he looked over at Beth. "Good morning, Detective...Crandall, was it?" He held out his hand and put on a new smile. "How can I help you? I see you're looking at our layouts. Can I interest you in buying into our outstanding community?"

She shook his hand. "It's tempting, for sure. You have some lovely homes here."

"Yes, and in a great range of prices, especially for all the amenities we include. Do you play golf? We have one award-winning course and a short course for those who aren't up to more than nine holes that day. If you'd like, I can arrange for you to play a round on us."

"Thanks anyway. I used to play but haven't for quite a while. Unfortunately, that's not what I'm here for today. I need to talk to you a bit more about Rita, if you can spare a few minutes."

"Sure. Anything I can do to help. Come on back into my office. May I get you some coffee, water, or a soda?"

"Nothing for me, thanks." Beth followed him down a short hall to a well-appointed office. The room was good sized, with a bookcase taking up most of one wall and containing what appeared to be numerous awards. Two of the other walls had attractive tropical pictures against a light sand-colored paint. The other wall was the attention-grabber. It boasted a large picture window overlooking a small natural-looking lake with woods beyond. A few white egrets picked their way along the shore, pecking at the ground as they looked for their brunch.

"Wow, I'd kill for a view like this." She laughed. "Well, not literally, since that would be very bad for the business I'm in."

Butch smiled and nodded as he looked around. "Yes, it's quite an eye-catching view, isn't it? You wouldn't believe how many people decide on a lot with a view of a lake or the woods because of what they see out this window."

Beth let out a little sigh. "Oh, I bet I can. My apartment has a view of the city, though, and that's pretty nice."

"Well, we'd love for you to consider living here with us. Having a resident police officer or detective could be nice. Needless to say, we'd hope you wouldn't have any more work to do here for an exceedingly long time, if ever."

"Thanks, I'll think about it." She reached into her jacket pocket for her notebook and pen. "You seem to be handling your wife's death well."

Butch sat in his desk chair and took a deep breath, letting it out in a sigh. He leaned forward, his elbows on his desk, his hands clasped. "First of all, I'm sure you've heard the rumors that Rita and I didn't exactly have the perfect marriage."

"Were they only rumors, or were you actually on the outs with each other?"

He looked up at the ceiling fan, appearing to contemplate the fake palm leaf-shaped blades as they slowly turned. He ran his hands over his face as he appeared to collect his thoughts. "Rita and I were on the verge of divorce. We've been that way for some time. We lived in the same house but led pretty much separate lives."

She nodded, making a couple of notes in her book. "So that's why you didn't report her missing?"

"Look, I know that sounds awful on the face of it, but she's gone off on her own somewhere before with no warning...even for several days at a time. I assumed that's what she did the other evening."

"I know you went over this right after we found Rita, but could you please tell me again about the last time you saw her?"

Butch looked at his hands before looking up at Beth. "It was the night of the big potluck. I believe I told you we always had one before most of the snowbirds came back as a kind of end of the off-season thing. Most of the people at the potluck were year-round residents. The population of this place triples during snowbird season. Anyway, as usual, Rita was drinking too much. I never knew why she even bothered to go to those things, since all she did was whine about how much she hated them. She'd get annoyed before she even left the house, although she always took something. She didn't cook much, so it was usually something she picked up from the deli department of the Publix down the road."

"Did anything unusual happen that night, other than her disappearance?"

Butch shook his head again. "Not that I remember, other than that she was drunk quicker than usual. I can tell you though, getting drunk at park gatherings was typical for her. That evening, for some reason, she decided to pick on a couple of the older ladies. She loudly made fun of one woman, Edith, for the way she dressed. Rita told Edith she should get a new outfit or two because she wore the same thing to every single event. She then said to please get something more stylish...even something from this century would be better."

Beth sat back in her chair. "Oh my..."

"Yeah, oh my, indeed. I was mortified. She's been bad before, but that was beyond bad, even for her. I went over and grabbed her by the arm, apologized to Edith when Rita wouldn't, and took her outside, away from the building. I tried to talk some sense into her and get her to knock it off. She kept ranting on about how I had moved her into an old people place, and she wasn't old—not by a long shot. Anyway, once we were outside, she got away from me and then staggered and stomped her way out onto the pier. I finally got her to sit down by promising her another drink if she'd stay put and shut up until I got back. I left her there on the dock sitting on a bench. That was the last I saw her alive."

"Do you remember about what time that was?"

"I'm not sure. Let's see, everyone had gone through the food line already, and some were on their seconds. I looked at the clock then and I seem to remember it being about seven. Events like that don't go on late here. They get their dinner, chat for a while, and they want to go home. Anyway, I'd been talking to someone about the upcoming golf tournament...shoot, I can't remember who that was. I heard Rita's voice from across the room and knew I had to go rescue poor Edith. That's when I grabbed Rita and took her outside. It couldn't have been much after seven. Maybe seven-fifteen? It was almost dark by the time we went outside."

"Hmm...did you see anyone else out there? I mean, anyone out on the lake or walking around on the clubhouse grounds?"

"I wasn't actually looking, to be truthful. Thinking about it now, I don't recall seeing anyone. I went back in the same door I took her out of." He chewed on his lower lip for a second. "On second thought, I do remember looking around to be sure no one heard her go off about living with old people. Rita always acted and dressed like she thought she was much younger than she was, but she and I are both several years over the younger age limit of fifty-five. I'm sure you couldn't fail to notice those weird neon pink sneakers she wore."

"Well, no, they were pretty hard to miss. Actually, I thought they were kind of cute."

Butch laughed. "To you, maybe. I thought they looked silly on her. I made the mistake of telling her what I thought when she came home with them."

Beth grimaced. "Uh, oh. Bad move, I bet."

"Yes, it was." He shook his head slowly, without looking away from her. "Just to get back at me, I'm sure, she wore them every time she got a chance. That was so annoying. It would've been one thing if she actually ran in them, but I don't think she ever ran anywhere a day in her life."

Beth made a note in her book. "Husbands often make that mistake. Wives, however, don't usually go to that extreme to get back at them. Were you two married long?"

He let out a long sigh. "Ten years this last spring. She was a widow when I met her."

"Do you know anything about her previous husband?"

"Not much. I understand he died a year or two before I met her. You know, if you want more information about her life before I met and married her, the person to ask is Kathy Blake. She and Rita have known each other for ages, long before Rita and I met. Those two have been thick as thieves since we moved in here...always up to something. Let me give you her contact information." He reached into his desk for a copy of the directory.

"I'll make a point of talking to her." Beth took down Kathy's phone number and address from Butch. "I'm sorry for your loss, and please forgive me for having to ask more questions."

"That's all right. I know you're only doing your job, and I appreciate that. Anything you need, just ask me. I want to find out how this happened, too."

"Thank you, I'm sure you do. Now, you did say you two were having some difficulties and thinking about divorce. Without being too intrusive, I do need to know what the nature of those difficulties was."

"It's no secret that Rita and I were having problems, mostly because of her excessive drinking and how Rita treated other people when she'd had too much. I'm sure she told her little group we were sleeping in separate bedrooms, which we were. To tell you the truth, I happen to be a bad snorer. It doesn't happen every night, but it's gotten worse over the last year or so. I should've had that checked out by a doctor, but I haven't gotten around to it. She couldn't sleep because of all the noise I made, so I started sleeping in the guest room. From what I heard, the most recent story she told her friends was that she didn't want to sleep with me anymore and kicked me out of our bedroom. That wasn't true at all. We weren't sleeping in the same bedroom so she could get some quiet."

Beth smiled, and then nodded as she made some notes. "That goes to show that you can't believe everything you hear around here, doesn't it? After so many years interviewing people, I can tell you that only about half of what people tell me, especially about other people, is entirely the truth. Sometimes it's all a lie, sometimes it's partially a lie, and sometimes it's because they're trying to protect someone, even if that someone is themselves."

Butch looked down at his desk blotter and managed a little smile. "What I just told you is all fact. I think maybe the people you talk to remember things wrong. Or maybe they remember them the way they want to or wish they were. In my case, I wish I could remember Rita in a better light." He put his elbows back on the desk, dropped his chin onto his hands and let out a small sigh. He turned a little silver-framed picture he had on his desk around for Beth to see. The photograph showed Butch and Rita cuddled together on a bench, his arm around her and her head on his shoulder. They were both smiling. "This was my Rita. It's how I choose to remember her. We used to be so much in love, and I'll always miss that Rita."

Chapter Fifteen

JESS BRUSHED HER HANDS over herself, trying to get as much yard debris off her t-shirt and cargo shorts as possible. She wiped her work boots on the doormat several times apiece before she knocked once, then three times, then once more on the door. Without waiting for an answer, she opened the door and climbed the three steps to let herself into her sister Joni's house. That distinctive knock was their little signal so Joni didn't need to get up from her crocheting projects and unsettle Max, her Cavalier King Charles Spaniel from his place next to her. Max used to jump up and bark when he heard her, and now the smart little guy knew that sound and didn't bother anymore.

"Well, hi, stranger." Joni put down the ocean blue baby blanket she was nearly finished with. "What brings you by today? Did you smell those cookies I made earlier?"

"Hi, sis. I'd give you a hug, but I don't think you want me anywhere near your latest project...or you, for that matter. I'll admit the aroma of your famous oatmeal cookies did get my attention while I was working nearby earlier. Got any left?"

"A few. Help yourself to the ones in the cookie jar. I'm saving the rest for the Screw Your Neighbor party this evening."

Jess felt her head snap back toward her sister. "Uh...what? Did I hear what I thought I heard?"

Joni laughed. "Oh, it's not what you think. It's a card party called Screw Your Neighbor. I guess someone should come up with a better name for it, but you'll have to admit it's an attention-getter. I went to a Screw Your Neighbor card party last week and had a lot of fun." She giggled. "You should've seen your face just now. I thought I was going to have to scrape your jaw up off the carpet."

"Did not. You surprised me, that's all. I've never heard of it. You'll have to admit the name does have a salacious sound to it."

"It's one of those games where you can do stuff to the person next to you. When someone first explained it to me, I immediately thought of all those Sorry games we played as kids. You got the biggest kick out of sending me backward as far as you could, then saying 'Sorry' in the most obnoxious voice you could manage."

"Hey, I was seven. It was the only way I could get back at you since you're eight years older. I was, however, awfully glad you deigned to spend time with your bratty little sister. You were usually an excellent big sister, I have to admit."

"Usually? Oh, come on. I was always a great big sister and still am."

"What about that time you were babysitting me and you had your boyfriend over? Remember him? The football player you were all gaga over?" Jess waggled her eyebrows and grinned.

Joni dramatically turned her eyes to the ceiling and sniffed. "I do not recall that incident."

"Uh huh, I'll bet you don't...especially since you married that hunky guy."

A smile lit up her face as she sighed. "I did...we had thirty-five wonderful years together. All right, now what brings you over here, other than a little trip down memory lane and the smell of cookies baking when you went by earlier?"

Jess put on the most innocent face she could muster. "Can't I just stop by to see my lovely sister?"

Joni looked over her reading glasses as she shook her head and pursed her lips.

"Not going for it?" Jess reached into the cookie jar for a couple of her favorites, found a napkin, and sat on a bar stool at the kitchen counter within sight of her sister. She made a point of staying far enough away to avoid dirtying up the furniture or carpet. "Okay, I was wondering if you've heard anything about this whole dead body in the lake thing. You're still active on the gossip circuit, aren't you?" She took a bite, holding it over the napkin to catch crumbs.

Joni made a couple more crochet stitches as she spoke. "I'm not nearly as well connected anymore as you think. I got tired of Bingo and the garden club ages ago. Why?"

"Oh, I was simply curious what you might've heard. My customers keep telling me all kinds of things, and the whole incident has been blown out of proportion."

"I'd say a dead body is a big deal, wouldn't you? People do die in here...I mean it's a senior community after all, but not like that. They usually die in their beds or drop dead in their yards."

Jess pointed a half-eaten cookie at her sister. "Of course, a dead body is always a big deal. I didn't mean to insinuate that it isn't. The silly stuff I'm hearing is about mob hits and bodies in every lake. This is pretty much a closed community. If someone did her in, it almost has to be someone in here. I have a hard time believing an outsider had anything to do with it."

"So, someone actually murdered Rita? I figured she fell into the lake, drunk again, and the alligators got her."

"The jury's still out on that, I guess. Or at least I'm not hearing anything more about it from Beth." As soon as she said it, she knew it was a mistake to mention Beth's first name.

"Wait...Beth? Beth who?" Joni dropped her crocheting project in her lap and took off her glasses, laying them on the coffee table. "I don't think I've heard you mention any Beth before."

Without taking her eyes off Joni, Jess took a bite of cookie, chewed and swallowed it before she answered. "Um...Beth Crandall, the detective on the case. Since I was the one that called it in from Edith's house, they had to interview me, too. Anyway, we kind of hit it off and now we're sort of friends."

"Kind of hit it off and sort of friends? What does that mean?" Joni grinned as she stared back at her. "This is sounding much more interesting than Dead Rita."

Jess waved her cookie dismissively. "It's not a big deal. Geez, I feel like a teenager being grilled by her mom."

"Sweetie, you haven't made a close friend since you moved up here. I'm happy you might've met someone who could be a real friend. You know, to talk to, hang out with, go out to dinner with, that kind of thing."

"What? Are you saying you don't want me hanging out around here eating all your baked goods?" Jess grinned, and then popped the last bite of cookie in her mouth.

"Sis, you're always welcome whenever you want to visit. I love having you live closer to me. We're the only family left now that Mom and Dad have both passed on. However, I've been hoping that you'd find a friend or two here your own age. Don't tell me some of your customers are your friends. Yes, they are, but they're mostly old enough to be your mom. You know, I'd love it if you found a companion. I also know how you feel about that, though."

Jess pressed her lips together and nodded slowly. "Yes, you do. I don't think I'm destined for a life partner, Joni. It's never worked out, and I've become quite content with things the way they are. I can come and go as I please, with whomever I please, or by myself if I please. I'm good with that. I do admit that I enjoy having Beth around to chat with. She invited herself over for a drink last week and she invited me over for dinner a couple of days ago. Nothing big. Sitting around talking, that's all. It's what I meant when I said what I did. Besides, I don't think she's my type."

"You mean, you don't know if she likes women, right?"

"That, and she's the modern furniture type, while I like the Old Florida laid-back style." Jess grinned. "She's a good cook, though."

"That's something you two have in common since you're not a bad cook yourself. Besides, you like to eat, too."

Jess shrugged. "That I do. Anyway, I don't know if it's going anywhere, and I don't care. We're simply enjoying each other's company. While this case is going on, we have something to talk about. After it's over, we may find we have nothing else in common and that will be that. I'm okay if that's what happens. I like having a friend right now."

"Sounds fair enough. All right, I'll let that go—for the time being." Joni sighed. "Now, back to Dead Rita. I don't know if it means anything, but I'm hearing that Rita was planning to ask Butch for a divorce. I believe I heard she had the real money in that marriage, but I don't see Butch killing her off. Do you?"

"Me? I didn't know either of them other than seeing them around. I think I spoke to Butch a few times when I was in the office for something, and that was it. He always seems pleasant...you know, friendly in a manager sort of way. Butch and Jackie seem to get along as coworkers. In fact, the whole office and sales crew seem to get along. Jackie never talks bad about any of them."

"Oh, that's Jackie. She likes everyone. She'd find something nice to say about a serial killer."

Jess made a little snorting noise. "You're so funny."

"No, really, I honestly think she would." Joni grinned at her. "She likes you a lot. Who wouldn't?"

"I do try to be nice. Anyway, even if Rita was going to ask Butch for a divorce, she'd most likely get no more than half of whatever they had, unless they had a prenup. At least that's what I understand. I don't know anything about that from personal experience."

"No, you wouldn't, having never been married or even in a relationship more than three years." Joni shook her head. "If Rita had a pile of money, though, you could bet she had a prenup."

Jess scrunched up her face at her. "But think about it. If Rita did in fact have a pile of money, do you think she'd live in Leisure Lakes? I'll admit this place is terrific and even on the upscale side for a retirement community, but...well...I guess I've always thought a wealthy person would prefer a house on some acreage."

"Jess, you're thinking like you. Not everyone wants the same things. Some quite well-off people buy homes in here. They've stopped wanting to take care of a large piece of property, and now they'd rather play golf every day. That's their idea of the perfect retirement. There are a lot of people in here like that, especially snowbirds. Some of those snowbirds still own amazing homes up north."

Jess thought for a second. "Point taken. Maybe Beth needs to see if Butch and Rita had an ironclad prenup agreement. I'd hate to think that he did it. I don't know why, but I didn't get the feeling that he could've faked that much shock when he saw Rita's body."

Joni picked up her crochet hook and pointed it at her. "Maybe not, and maybe what I told you isn't important. Anyway, I hope they leave George alone. There's no way he killed Rita."

"I agree. Besides, unless they want to check all the bite marks of all the bigger alligators in here, they couldn't prove which one took a bite and then spit it out on Edith's yard." Jess laughed. "I guess Rita was so nasty that even the gators didn't want her."

That got Joni to chuckle a bit before frowning. "No, but they could decide to remove every alligator in here that's big enough to have bitten off the leg. I know they don't kill them, but we like George and want to keep him until he's too big to live here. He's no nuisance at all, unlike Rita."

Jess laughed again. "He's no nuisance to you, anyway. Remember that time I was working in your front yard and your buddy George decided to come see what I was doing while my back was turned? If it hadn't been for Sam from down the street happening to pass by in his car, I might've backed right into those jaws without knowing. Thank goodness he kept blowing his horn until I heard him over the music in my earbuds."

Joni shook her head. "Yep, you were almost a nuisance to George. You did get some great pictures of him, after you moved out of range of those jaws. Still, I don't think he was trying to bite you. More than likely, he was fascinated with what you were doing."

"Right. I've kept an eye out for him, that's for sure. I'd rather neither of us is a nuisance to the other one."

Joni put her glasses back on and picked up the baby blanket, pulling some yarn from the neatly wound ball next to her on the sofa. "I just don't think George is the killing type, unless he saw something as food." She looked over her glasses as she pointed her crochet hook at Jess again and grinned. "Or unless he saw something as a threat, like you."

Chapter Sixteen

THAT EVENING AFTER DINNER found Jess back out on her porch, listening to the whooshing of the tree branches in the light breeze and the scratching of squirrels running up the trunks. A yummy aroma wafted her way—the telltale sign that someone down the street was grilling a steak outside. Smiling, she once again congratulated herself on having a near perfect life. Too bad everyone couldn't be that content—there'd be far less crime, let alone murder.

Jess found herself pondering the circumstances that could drive a person to kill another human being. In her experience, it was usually someone who knew the deceased well. There were many reasons for it, and all of them bad but one. The only one she could sort of understand was the mercy killing of a spouse or parent because they were in horrible, incurable pain. Situations of that sort made her at least try to understand the whole assisted suicide thing. But this wasn't one of those. Rita appeared to be in good health and had been out doing what she usually did–getting drunk and annoying people, not necessarily in that order.

The murder victim's spouse was almost always the first suspect, and she knew Beth was doing a thorough investigation of that situation. If Rita did have most of the money in that relationship, and she was getting ready to divorce Butch, well, she'd seen money as a motive for lots of crimes. The fact that it was hard to see Butch as a murderer was meaningless. Some of the worst cases were those who came off as completely innocent from the get-go and looked like they'd hardly swat a fly.

There had to be others who would've liked to get rid of Rita, but killing her took something extra. Besides, Leisure Lakes was huge. If someone didn't want to be around her, they didn't need to be anywhere near her, pretty much.

She asked herself, *Okay, playing around with what ifs, what if this whole thing turned out to be an accident? What if she did simply fall into the lake after too much alcohol? Wouldn't hitting the water rouse her enough to get out of the lake? Beth said there were tiny bits of wood in a head wound. How hard would she have had to hit her head to knock herself out?*

Another thing bothered Jess. That lake wasn't exceptionally deep right off the dock, maybe chest height to the average grown man. Most adults could stand up and walk out of the water there, even if they had to tread water part of the way. Why didn't she do just that if she fell off drunk? She could've staggered back onto the shore and collapsed there.

Something is missing. What is it? Jess scratched her head. She felt like her brain was running hard as if on a treadmill, getting nowhere. This wasn't her case. Her saying nowadays was 'not my circus, not my monkeys.' None of this was her problem. She wasn't the detective and didn't want to be anymore. Why was she so caught up with it? It should all be left to the official detective and her officers.

Beth. Detective Beth. Detective Crandall, that is. With the auburn hair and funny laugh. Yes, she's more than likely the real attraction to this case. To add to that, her customers were always talking about it. Dead Rita truly was more of a conversation item than Live Rita ever was.

All right, now. What if it wasn't Butch? Who in Leisure Lakes would've hated her enough to want her dead? There was probably a long list of people who disliked her. There might even have been a few 'ding dong the witch is dead' parties, a la *The Wizard of Oz*. Actually killing her, that's another matter. Rita must've done something especially nasty to someone if they took the effort to murder her.

Rita had totally humiliated Edith at that potluck. But Edith was close to ninety years old and was no match at all for Rita, even a drunk one. Besides, according to what she'd heard, Edith had merely sat there and taken it, then started to cry a little. Nope, it can't be Edith.

Butch had been seen coming back in and a while later, he said he went back out to check on Rita. He probably could've killed her the first time and faked going back out there to set up an alibi, or he could've done it the second time he went out there and pretended she wasn't there anymore. Without any witnesses, who knows what happened.

Her head started to hurt. She began repeating, "Not my monkeys, not my circus," over and over. One thing she felt she knew for sure was that was not a random act of violence. She didn't have to worry about her sister living alone out at Leisure Lakes. Rita was most likely done in by someone who knew her.

Chapter Seventeen

THE NEXT MORNING, AS she started her pickup to go to work, Jess heard her phone go off. Her thumb punched the answer button before she looked to see who it was.

"Hey Jess!" said the male voice on the other end. "Do you think you could stop by my place before you start work? I want to run something by you."

It took Jess a few seconds to realize who it was. The voice belonged to Ben Roswell, a former customer that she hadn't seen or talked with since last spring when he went back north for the summer. She didn't have many snowbirds as customers. She and Ben had hit it off when she first started working in Leisure Lakes and had remained friendly since then.

"Ben! You're back! Great to hear from you. I'll be happy to stop by. Do you want to give me a clue about what's going on? If not, it's all right. I can be there inside of fifteen minutes."

"To tell you the truth, I'd rather not talk about it over the phone. I need your advice about something that you might help me with, given your police background. I'll have coffee ready. I'll see you in a few minutes. And Jess...thank you." She heard a click and he was gone.

Okaaaaay. That was interesting, she thought. *He's asked for advice about bushes or weed killer or the like but never anything like this before.*

Exactly thirteen minutes later, Jess parked her pickup in Ben's driveway. She had plenty of room behind the car parked there—a red 2001 or so Toyota Corolla. A widower, Ben still had the car his wife used to drive and it appeared immaculate as always. She remembered hearing him say he'd keep it until it fell apart because it reminded him of her. Since he was pushing ninety hard, it was entirely possible he'd fall apart before that car did. Jess thought it was sweet that he loved his wife so much.

Before Jess got to the door, Ben—always big on handshakes—came down the steps with his hand out. A big man, he still had tons of steel grey hair, wore one of those tropical button-up shirts every day, and had a smile that lit up his whole face. One hand in the handshake, the other on her shoulder, that was his regular greeting to her.

"Gretchen's car still looks great, doesn't it?" Ben paused to admire the red car with her. "She's got over 150,000 miles on her now, and she still runs fantastic. She still looks pretty, too, don't you think?"

Jess grinned and gave a little pat to the hood. "She sure does. You take great care of her. Now, did you mention something about coffee?"

"As a matter of fact I did, didn't I? Come on in. I just made a fresh pot."

A few minutes later, Ben and Jess were sitting at the table in the breakfast nook, sipping from their mugs and chatting about the neighbors and others they both knew. Jess was always amazed at what a quiet man this big guy was. Ben's wife had passed on before Jess met him and she'd always wondered if he'd been different when his wife was alive.

After a bit of small talk, Ben put his coffee mug down and looked at her intently. "I'm sure you're curious why I wanted your opinion about something having to do with police business, right?"

"Curious is putting it mildly. You've never asked me anything about that kind of thing before—never shown much interest. What's up, Ben?"

He picked up his spoon, stirred his coffee absently, and looked up at her again. "I know I saw something and I'm not sure what it was. It might have something to do with the manager's wife dying, but I don't want to cause anyone to get into trouble if it was really nothing. Know what I mean?"

Jess nodded slowly. "I do."

"This is hard for me. I don't claim to know the people I saw, and I didn't know the manager's wife, either."

"The woman who died was named Rita. I figured everyone knew her."

He looked back down at his cup. "Nah, I've stayed away from most of the goings-on in this place. When we bought our house, I wanted a warm place to spend my winters and a yard to putter around in, that's pretty much it. I'm not one for hanging out at the clubhouse or going to the dances or the like. I'm not interested in being hit on by the women in here, either. There will never be another woman in my life after my Gretchen." He looked back up at Jess. "You're the sole female friend I have. I guess I don't think of you much as a woman, just a friend in general. No offense meant."

Jess laughed. "None taken. I take it as a compliment that you think of me as a friend. Period."

"Good. That's how I meant it. Anyway, I was out in my golf cart the night they had that big potluck at the clubhouse. I returned to Leisure Lakes a couple of days prior, and I was taking a little ride around to see what was new. I stopped and parked over by the lake, pretty much right across the water from the clubhouse. I sat there enjoying the view for a bit, then I noticed some people out on the clubhouse dock."

"Okay. What caught your attention? Could you tell what was going on? Did you recognize them?"

"No, I didn't recognize either of them. As a matter of fact, I couldn't even tell you if they were male or female because it looked like both were wearing shorts or pants—not dresses or skirts, anyway. There were two of them, though, and they appeared to be arguing."

"What made you think they were arguing?"

"From where I was, I could hear faint voices. The breeze must've carried the sound over. I couldn't hear what they were saying, but it looked like they were waving their arms around, as if they were having a heated argument about something. They appeared to be pointing or had their hands out toward each other...and not for a hug. One of them pushed the other one and the other one shoved back."

"Do you know about what time that was?"

"Not really. It was getting dark and I didn't think to look at my watch. I wouldn't have seen anything at all if the clubhouse hadn't been lit up. I wasn't doing anything but sitting there, and I happened to notice them. I didn't think too much about it until I heard about Rita."

"All right. Did you notice what happened next? I mean, did they stay out there, or did they go inside?"

"It looked like whatever was going on, it must've come to a draw. They were both still waving their arms around and it looked like one was pointing at the other, from where I sat. One of them gave another shove and it looked like the other one swung something. Then it looked like they fell or sat down or something because I didn't see them fighting anymore. After that, it looked like the person who swung something held their hand up and pointed at the other one again like they were saying something, and then they walked away."

"What about the other one?"

"I couldn't see them. I assumed they were sitting on the bench or on the dock. I decided I'd seen enough of what was most likely a drunken fight, and I drove away. When I drove past again about twenty minutes later, I glanced over there and didn't see anyone, but by then it was dark. I assumed whatever it was, it was all over. To tell you the truth, I was relieved. That kind of stuff is why I don't go to the events and dinners here. Seems like someone always gets drunk and makes a scene."

"By someone, do you mean Rita? Or have others caused a ruckus as well?"

"I don't know much about who does stuff like that now. I do remember the manager's wife getting into it with people when I used to go, and partly because of that, it's been several years since I bothered. If I want to enjoy dinner with someone nowadays, I invite them over to my house or meet them at the clubhouse restaurant."

"Got it. Well, what's your question for me, then?"

Ben took a deep breath and let it out slowly. "I need to know if I should let the police know what I saw. I mean, I can't identify either of them, but I did see something."

"I think you should talk to the detective in charge of the investigation. She's easy to talk to, and what you're telling me might be useful to her case. You never know what little piece of information will turn out to be helpful in ruling someone in or out as a suspect," she said, taking Beth's card out of her card case. "Here's her number. Would you like it?"

Ben took a sip of his coffee and put the mug back on the table before answering. "I know this makes me sound kind of silly, but do you mind calling for me? I don't know what to tell her."

Jess reached over and patted him on the arm. "You don't sound silly at all. I'll pass the phone to you or put her on speaker if you like and you can talk to her yourself once she knows what it's about. How's that?"

He nodded. "That sounds good. Can we call her now and get it over with?"

"Sure. She should be at work. And, by the way, from what I've seen of her, I think you'll like her."

"I'm sure I will. But if she needs to come here and talk to me, do you think you could be here with me? I'm not used to dealing with the police. Having you here would make me feel better about talking to her."

"I'll call right now if you'd like me to. I'm sure you'll be fine. You only need to tell her what you told me and let her decide whether what you saw is useful. She'll probably ask you some questions, but nothing you'll have trouble answering. How does that sound?"

Ben gave her a little smile through pressed lips. "That sounds good. It's just that I don't want to get anyone in trouble, especially if what I saw was, in fact, no big deal."

Jess took her phone from her shorts pocket and began punching in Beth's number. "As I said, you might actually help get someone out of trouble. You never know."

After a couple of rings, Beth picked up with her usual, "Hi Jess! What's up?"

"Good morning, detective. I've someone here who has some information about that case you're working on out at Leisure Lakes. If it's okay, I'd like to put you on speaker."

"No problem on this end. Hit the button and let's all chat."

"Okay." Jess hit the speaker button and placed her phone on the table between herself and Ben. "Detective Beth Crandall, please meet Mr. Ben Roswell. He saw something that might be helpful to your case, and we thought you should hear about it."

Beth's voice was as friendly as a handshake. "Happy to meet you, Mr. Roswell. Would you like to tell me what you saw and when?"

Jess put her hand on Ben's shoulder and nodded.

Ben looked back at Jess, then at the phone. "I just got back to Leisure Lakes a day or two before this all happened. The evening they had that big potluck at the clubhouse, I was driving around in my golf cart for a little ride. I stopped on the opposite side of the lake from the clubhouse. It was a pleasant evening and I was enjoying the cool breeze. I don't know exactly when it was, but it was getting dark."

"All right, Mr. Roswell. What exactly is it that you saw or heard?"

"Some voices caught my attention. They sounded like they came from the other side of the lake. When I looked hard, I could make out two people on the pier in front of the clubhouse."

"Could you see who they were or what they were doing?"

"I don't know who they were. I couldn't see that clearly, truth be told. I did hear two voices and it sounded like they were arguing from the tone of them. It looked like one of them was waving their arms around and pointing at the other one."

"Did you hear anything at all of what they were saying?"

"No, not really. I couldn't even be sure if they were male or female, although their voices seemed to carry across the lake about the same." Ben glanced over at Jess again then back at the phone. "If I had to hazard a guess, I'd say they were both female, but I wouldn't swear to it."

"And you couldn't hear any of what they were saying?"

"Not a single word. From where I sat it was only noise, like those grown-up voices on the Charlie Brown cartoons. I'm sorry I can't be more help on that."

"That's okay. Could you see what they were doing?"

"Like I said, they were waving their arms around like they were arguing, and it looked like there was some pushing and shoving going on, and one of them looked like they swung something. The other one appeared to get pushed or knocked down...either onto the dock or onto the bench. I didn't hear a splash, so I'm guessing the one that went down didn't fall into the lake. The other one reached down and either pointed or poked at something, then appeared to walk away. At that point, I decided to leave."

"Actually, Mr. Roswell, what you're telling me is valuable information. Could I have your address and phone number in case I need to ask you anything else?"

"I guess so. I can't imagine what else I saw that could be helpful, but I'm happy to help any way I can."

Chapter Eighteen

BETH PULLED UP IN front of 4817 Queen Palm Loop, one of the biggest homes in Leisure Lakes. A grouping of three palms surrounded by well-trimmed hibiscus bushes commanded the center of the front lawn. The triple wide manufactured home, plus its two-car carport, took up most of the generous double lot the home sat on. Since it was on a cul-de-sac, Beth guessed they had a huge back yard. She walked slowly to the door, using up another minute so she'd be exactly on time according to her watch.

The doorbell sounded like chimes from a bell tower, and seconds later a smiling Kathy Blake came to the door. A petite woman with pixie-cut light brown hair, she was dressed in golf attire—a lavender polo shirt and coordinating skort.

Kathy offered her hand for a handshake. "My goodness, you're certainly on time, aren't you?"

"I try," Beth said, accepting the handshake.

Kathy waved her in. "Welcome to our home. Can I get you some coffee? I just made a fresh pot."

"I'd love some coffee. Thank you."

On the way to the lanai, Kathy introduced Beth to her husband, Ed. He smiled and shook hands then made himself scarce, saying he was sure they'd like some privacy to talk. A few minutes later, they were settled on the lanai overlooking that large back yard Beth had suspected was there.

Beth took a sip from her coffee. "What a wonderful view you have. It looks like a great place to entertain."

"We love it. That potential view was what sold us on moving here. When we bought into Leisure Lakes, it was nowhere near as full of homes as it is now. We had most of this cul-de-sac to ourselves. The lake to the left and the woods off to the right give us a view of nearly everything but the golf course. We're good with that, though. Have you ever lived on a golf course?"

"Can't say that I have."

"Let's just say that you need to be prepared to fix a lot of broken windows and keep a repair company on speed dial. Golf courses are a great view, but no thank you ever again. We're happy with the lake and the woods."

"It's truly lovely here. Let me know if you ever decide to move. I'd love to get up every day to this view."

Kathy smiled sweetly. "If we have anything to do with it, it'll be a long time before we leave here. If that changes, we'll keep you in mind. Now, you mentioned on the phone that you wanted to ask me about Rita." She picked up her china cup from its matching saucer, taking a sip from her coffee.

"I did." Beth pulled her notebook and pen out of her bag. "First of all, let me extend my condolences. I understand you and Rita were close friends for quite a while?"

Kathy placed her coffee cup on its saucer with a little clinking sound. "Yes, we were, poor thing. We got to know each other back when we were young and married to our first husbands, who had been friends since childhood. Sadly, they both died. When we remarried, our new husbands didn't know each other and had their own families and friends, and as couples, we drifted apart. We found each other again when Butch took over managing Leisure Lakes."

"Wow, that must've been a surprise. I mean, what were the chances that would happen?"

Kathy nodded. "I know. It was quite a surprise since I hadn't heard from her at all for several years. It was wonderful to see Rita again and be able to do things together."

"I'm sure it was. Did she seem like the same person that you remembered? Or had she changed in some way?" Beth put her hand up before Kathy could answer. "I'm simply looking for some insight into the person Rita was."

"I understand. Well, no, she wasn't quite the same. She was moodier, for one thing. And I'm sure you've heard that she drank a lot, especially lately."

"I'd heard that, but you know how rumors are."

"It wasn't a rumor. She did drink—a lot. The Rita I used to know wasn't like that. A glass or two of wine in the evening was about it as far as what I saw. Since she moved here, it seemed like every afternoon about three she'd have that first one. Sometimes she'd even have one or more at lunch, and she wasn't sipping a glass of wine, like the rest of us. Sometimes she'd hit the hard stuff early in the day, too." Kathy sighed. "I wish she hadn't. It wasn't very pretty."

"What do you mean?"

"There were times when she and Butch got into it after she'd had a few, and she'd come over here and hole up in our guest room for a day or two. At some point, she'd leave without a word and apparently they'd make up."

Beth made a note in her notebook. "Was there ever any indication that he put hands on her, like hit her for instance, when they 'got into it' as you said?"

"Butch?" She shook her head. "Oh no. He wasn't like that. They usually got into shouting matches and she'd stomp off, slamming doors like a teenager. If there was any hitting going on, I'm sure she was the one who hit him. I sort of felt sorry for him."

"What do you mean?"

Kathy looked down at her coffee cup briefly and back up at Beth. "When she drank a lot, she could get mean."

"I see. Was she drinking that night at the clubhouse potluck?"

Kathy pursed her lips and nodded.

"A lot?"

Kathy nodded again. "I wasn't watching how many she had, but that night she was fairly plastered, worse than I'd ever seen her."

"And was she acting nasty again?"

"Yes, even more than usual. That night for, no apparent reason, she was going around the room picking on people. I think the final straw for Butch was when Rita went over to a lady named Edith. Everyone knows Edith. She's a sweet woman—in her late eighties, I'd guess. Now, even though Edith had never done anything to Rita, that didn't stop her. Rita started making fun of her clothes, telling her she should get something from this century, or the like."

Beth shook her head. "That's pretty rude, for sure."

"Look, I'm Rita's friend, or was, but I was glad to see Butch take her outside. I didn't intervene myself because Rita would've started in on me, friend or no friend. I wish now that I'd taken her home with me and let her rant it out. Ed wouldn't have liked it, that's for sure, after the way she acted. He can't stand her. I probably could've gotten her into bed in the guest room and let her sleep it off. If I had, maybe she'd still be alive." She reached for her cup and took another sip.

"So, the last time you saw her was when Butch took her outside?"

"No, it wasn't. When Butch left with her, I assumed he was taking her straight home. When he came back in without her, I asked how she was. He told me she'd thrown a fit outside and he'd left her out on the pier. He said he was going to let her stew for a bit. I decided to go out and sit with her."

Beth made a couple of notes on her notepad. "Okay, what happened after that? What was she doing when you went out to sit with her?"

"I found her sitting on one of the benches on the pier, talking to herself."

"Talking to herself? That couldn't have been a good thing."

"No, it wasn't. I barely sat down beside her when she jumped up and started yelling at me for no reason. I mean, I'm her best friend, and that behavior was totally uncalled for. I did try to calm her down, even though she was having none of it."

"Did you stay with her till Butch came back out?"

"No. She was acting so horrid, I'd had enough. I admit I did push her once when she acted like she was going to hit me. I couldn't believe it—me, of all people. She was so drunk she staggered backward against the bench and sat down hard. I told her she could sit out there by herself, and I turned around and went back to the clubhouse. I didn't even look back. I assumed Butch was going to take her home later and she'd sleep it off there."

"Was Butch coming out when you went back in?"

"No. I didn't see him on my way back."

"Did you see anyone else out there when you were with Rita?"

"I wasn't looking around, to tell the truth. When I went out, I was focused on Rita. When I went back in, I was so mad at her that all I could think about was going inside, getting my husband, and heading home. What I did notice when I got back in was that quite a few people were talking to Edith. I could hear them saying how sorry they were for how Rita acted. I guess I should've said something to her, too. We aren't friends, though, and she looked like she had plenty of people around to console her."

Beth nodded. "I understand. You didn't see Rita again after you left her on the pier?"

"No, I didn't."

"What about Butch? Did you see him again after that?"

"Yes, I saw him talking to some people after I came back into the clubhouse. I guess I should've said something to him so he'd know she was out there alone, but I didn't."

"You didn't leave right away?"

"No, we didn't. Ed said there was no point in leaving now that Rita wasn't spoiling the party anymore, but we didn't stay long after that. I just wanted to go home. The whole thing was ruined for most of us, so it was a good thing we'd already had dinner. Ed brought me home, but he forgot something and had to go back to look for it. He wasn't gone long."

"How did Butch seem?"

"Butch seemed normal. He'd seen Rita drunk enough times, I'm sure it no longer fazed him. People kept coming up to him to talk, so he didn't go back outside again while I was still there. Why do you ask?"

"Just curious. I'm trying to make a timeline of what happened when and who might've seen her last. Was it common for Rita to wander off somewhere for a couple of days when she went on a bender or was mad at him?"

"Yes, and she usually landed at my house. Like I said, my husband wasn't exactly a fan of hers. He's a patient guy and he understood that Rita and I had been friends for years before he met me. I'm fortunate that he usually put up with it without a word...just some dirty looks. Occasionally, he said he wished I'd stop hanging around with her, and he tried to get me to make her leave a few times before she was ready. That's as far as it went. I guess he's happy now that she's gone. He hasn't missed her, that's for sure."

"I'm sure he's not happy your friend is dead, but he could be relieved that you don't need to deal with her anymore. I'm sure it wasn't always fun for you or him, either. I mean, who did you talk to about your issues with Rita when she was your best friend?"

"I do have other people to talk to in here, especially since I've been living in Leisure Lakes much longer than she has. Sometimes I confided in one of them when I needed to. Of course, whoever I talked to was sworn to secrecy since I didn't want to spread rumors about Rita. She was the manager's wife."

"You're a good friend. It does seem that gossip is a hot commodity in every community after all."

Kathy rolled her eyes and nodded. "Especially here. It's amazing what I'm hearing about the night poor Rita died. I mean, a mob hit for goodness sake!"

"Let me ask you this: when you didn't see or hear from Rita for a couple of days after the potluck, did you call Butch or ask around about her?"

Kathy shook her head slowly as she answered. "No, I didn't. I know it sounds awful, but I didn't. It sometimes took her a couple of days to settle down. Besides, she'd been quite belligerent toward me when I last saw her, and I assumed she was still mad at me. As close as we were, I was kind of glad to have a few quiet days after that. I'd already decided I was going to call her or Butch the day they found her body." She looked down and ran her finger over the handle of the coffee cup. "I'll never forget hearing how they found her."

Beth put her hand softly on Kathy's arm. "That must've been awful for you, hearing about your friend like that."

"It was. When we heard about that leg thing, I sure didn't put two and two together and come up with Rita. It wasn't until later that I heard about those running shoes she was wearing. It's not like she was the only one in here that wore those things, although she was probably the only one who wore them just for a fashion statement."

"And she was wearing them the night of the potluck?"

"Seems like I do remember her wearing them. She wore them a lot, mostly because Butch hated them." Kathy leaned forward. "To tell you the truth, I'm quite sure she did it out of spite. It probably started out because she saw someone running in them and thought they were cute. She went on wearing them so much mostly because Butch told her they looked silly on her and she should act her age. That's what usually set her off, you know—Butch telling her to act her age."

"I see. Did she fancy herself as much younger?"

"I don't think she saw herself past her thirties. She kept her hair colored and maintained her weight small enough to shop in the junior department. That way she could wear those skinny jeans and other things that young people wear. I'm sure that's what those shoes represented, too."

"I hope you don't think this is intrusive, but I've heard a rumor that she and Butch were thinking about divorcing. I've also heard they were sleeping in separate bedrooms."

"Oh, she talked about that off and on. They originally started sleeping in separate bedrooms because Rita couldn't stand his snoring. I got the impression that Butch has some kind of breathing issue. I remember she told me she wished he'd see a doctor about it because she was sure he had sleep apnea. Lately, she started telling me that he wasn't a considerate lover and he just wanted what he wanted and afterward he'd go back to his room. I don't know how true that was. Rita wasn't above making up elaborate tales about things. It's possible she was thinking about divorce. She never actually said the D word, though."

"Was she financially dependent on him or did she have her own money?"

"She had her own. When her first husband died, he left her a large insurance policy and an expansive home that was paid off. Not long after he died, she sold the house and bought a condo. She was well provided for, that's for sure. I can't imagine she's gone through all of that already. From what I understand, Butch has money of his own, and I'm sure he makes an excellent salary here. So, no, I don't think they stayed together for financial reasons. I did often wonder if she stopped loving him but stayed married to him because she didn't want to be alone again. From what I saw, Rita and Butch looked like they were very much in love when they first got together."

Beth made some notes in her notebook. "I see. How long was she on her own after her first husband died?"

"About two years. She kept saying that there was no one like her first husband, and she'd say that she'd never remarry. By the time she met Butch, I believe she was tired of living alone."

Beth made a couple of notations in her notebook. "Were you around them when she and Butch first married?"

"Oh yes, I was at their wedding. Like I said, they seemed happy and in love. I was so pleased for her. She wasn't the kind to live the rest of her life alone, and I was glad she found such a nice man. I don't know what happened that made her so different." Kathy leaned a little closer and lowered her voice. "Maybe she had mental issues or something. I have no idea. I've stayed friends with her since she moved here because we'd been connected for so long that I didn't want to give up on her." A little tear trickled down her cheek, and she reached for a tissue to dab at it.

Beth took that as her cue to leave. "Listen, I don't want to take any more of your time. Thanks for the coffee and again, I'm sorry you lost your friend."

Kathy sniffed again and dabbed her nose. "Thank you. If there's anything else I can do, please let me know."

Beth handed her one of her business cards. "If you think of anything else that might help us figure this out, please give me a call. You've given me some useful information."

She dabbed at her eye once more. "I'm glad I could help in some way."

"Oh, one more thing. Did she usually carry a handbag or the like?"

"Not a regular handbag. She owned several, but unless we were going to do some major shopping, she usually carried a little shoulder bag big enough for her phone and some money or cards, and that's all. It was more like an overgrown pocket. Why do you ask?"

"We haven't found her phone yet. Was she carrying that little bag the night of the potluck?"

Kathy seemed to think for a few seconds. "I couldn't swear to it, one way or the other. I don't remember."

"Do you remember what that little bag she usually carried looked like?"

"Yes, it was small, black, with a little flap that went over the zipper on top and snapped on the front. It was a cross-body style with a skinny strap. It wasn't an expensive designer bag like she usually had, she found it somewhere and just liked how it looked. I warned her several times that the strap was almost like a string and too easy to break. That it didn't break is amazing. She wore that thing all over, like a piece of clothing."

"I'd like to ask you one other thing. Did she keep a calendar on her phone? Like a datebook?"

"I'm sure she did. She was quite particular about being somewhere if she said she was going to. Why do you ask?"

"We didn't find her phone or her bag with her."

"That's odd. Like I said, she wore that bag everywhere, and she was never far away from her phone."

Chapter Nineteen

BETH WATCHED AS A police diver sloshed around in the water under and around the Leisure Lakes clubhouse pier. It was mid-morning and even though it was technically still fall, it was getting quite warm as she stood in the sun. As she removed her blazer and draped it over the pier post, she noticed a small group of golf carts gathering on the other side of the lake. It was obvious the locals were keeping an eye on the goings-on.

The diver was feeling around for a small black item in the water under the dock. Because the water level varied a lot during the year, that area was choked with grass and other growth. There was no way to see well, even with a snorkel and mask. After nearly an hour, he took a break and jumped up on the pier to sit.

"Well?" Beth handed him a bottle of water.

He shrugged as he opened the bottle and took a long swig of the cold water. "It's hard to see anything at all. The sand on the bottom is dark, too. With all those grasses and the like growing in there, I'll be surprised if we find anything."

"You paid special attention to the area I pointed out? Where they found the body?"

"I did exactly as you told me. I went twenty feet in all directions. If that bag's in this lake, it's not near the pier. It's possible someone threw it out farther or a gator dragged it away. I'll widen the search in a minute."

"Thanks. I don't want to have to drag this whole lake for a tiny handbag."

He grinned. "You and me both. It wouldn't be fun."

Another half hour of searching and still nothing. She watched him methodically search in a grid pattern, moving from one area to another when nothing was found. Although she had other things to do besides wait on the pier, she couldn't tear herself away from it. She wanted to be there if he found it. It was quite pleasant out there, once she removed her jacket. Besides, someone had to be the lookout for alligators while the diver carried out his search.

A second break on the pier and another bottle of water, and the diver went back into the water right where he left off. A couple of times he thought he found something, only to have it turn out to be some odd piece of detritus left by the local fishermen. If something was accidentally dropped overboard in this lake, it appeared no one bothered going in after it. Then again, when the average age is mid-seventies or above, it was possible they didn't feel it was worth it. It was also possible they didn't want to take a chance on annoying any alligator that could be hanging around. The only other things he found were beer bottles and an old baseball bat. He brought up the bat just for the fun of it and laid it on the pier, where they made jokes about fishermen beating up the fish with it in between all the beers they were drinking.

"How much longer do you want me to do this?" he asked on the third break. "I'm willing to give it another try, but much more than that and we're going to need more help. Besides, I don't want to attract the attention of any of the local alligators."

Beth let out a long low sigh. "Yes, I know. This might be a fool's errand looking for that tiny handbag. Her husband didn't have it and it wasn't on her body. I hoped maybe it came off when she fell in and would've been fairly close to the pier." She stared off at the other end of the lake as she thought for a minute. "It's possible someone snatched it and either took it with them or, like you mentioned, threw it farther out into the lake. I don't see any reason for that. She apparently didn't keep much in it—a little money, a card, and her phone. Nothing much worth stealing."

He laughed. "Maybe her phone had some sexy text messages on it from a lover and he didn't want it found?"

"From what I've heard about her, it's hard to believe anyone would send her messages of that sort, but I'll keep that in mind. Tell you what, one more time into the lake, and if you don't find it, we'll give it up for now. How about that?"

He gave a thumbs-up, downed the rest of his water, and jumped back in. Five minutes later, he came up, tore off his snorkel, and yelled, "Bingo!" He held up a small dripping black bag that looked like their target.

Beth was waiting for him on the dock with an evidence bag. She couldn't wait to see if it really was Rita's. It looked the right size as Kathy had described it. When the diver reached the dock, she nearly snatched it from him.

"Brendan, if this is what it looks like it is, I'll buy you lunch," she said, taking the dripping thing.

"You bet. I'll take you up on that!" He grinned as he launched himself out of the water and onto the pier, keeping his eyes on Beth's prize.

Beth held it away from her to keep from getting wet. There were what looked like bite marks on the outside, so some alligator probably tried it as a snack and discarded it. She unzipped it and looked inside. Sure enough, not much in there but a cell phone. Thank goodness the phone was there. She laid the bag down on the evidence bag sitting on the pier bench as she cataloged its contents: One iPhone of some variety with a bright red cover on it, forty-five dollars in cash, a soggy tissue, a key ring with three keys, and a little hard-sided case that people usually carry cards in. Pushing the button on the case, it clicked open, revealing the owner's driver's license right there in front.

"Yes! It's Rita's!" she said to Brendan, holding it up like a trophy. "Looks like I owe you that lunch and I'm ready to pay up whenever you're ready. You've earned it."

"I'm going to hold you to that when this case is solved. Do you think the phone still works?"

"Possibly. These new phones are somewhat waterproof, so it's possible something might be retrievable from it. I'd better leave it alone until someone who knows more than I do can be sure I don't fry the connections inside. From the looks of the bag contents, though, robbery wasn't a motive. The cash and cards are still here."

"That means..."

"Yep, it was probably someone who knew her. Although, if it had been me, I would've taken the phone and destroyed it, then put it out for the trash in a dumpster somewhere."

Brendan laughed. "I can see you've thought this through. Are you planning to do someone in?"

Before she could reply, they heard a splash from the other side of the lake. The diver yanked his legs out of the water and stood up on the pier. "Wow! I got out just in time. That one looked like a juvenile, but still..."

"You're right. I didn't even see it. Some lookout I was. I wouldn't want you to become an alligator snack, too."

Chapter Twenty

TWO DAYS LATER, THE lab called Beth to say the phone was dried out. It didn't stay on long. It had been underwater for several days and was soaked with lake water. They downloaded everything they could from it as quickly as possible, but they couldn't guarantee anything useful. She had them send whatever they got to her work computer.

As soon as it came up, she noticed something in Rita's recent call history. It was a noticeably short call a few weeks ago to a local phone number that wasn't one of Rita's gaggle of cronies. Rita had put the number in her contacts, labelling it just as GS with a four-digit number after it. It was also odd that Rita hadn't deleted that one from her recent calls. She'd left it there in her call history.

She called Butch to see if he knew one of her friends with those initials, but he didn't. Next a call to Kathy with the same question, and again the answer was no. Finally, she called Butch back and asked him if he could look through the resident directory for anyone with those initials. He found one: Gabriella Singleton. He gave her Mrs. Singleton's phone number but said he was sure Rita didn't know her.

The phone numbers matched. The initials matched. The next thing was to contact her and see if she knew anything. She got Mrs. Singleton's voice mail and left a message asking when she could come over and talk to her. An hour later, there was a return call apologizing and saying she had been playing golf. Mrs. Singleton said she'd be home in about half an hour and would be happy to see her. She gave Beth her address and said she'd see her then.

That was when she noticed that the other number was Mrs. Singleton's house number. Not the street name, only the house number. Something else odd.

Chapter Twenty-one

GABRIELLA SINGLETON LIVED IN the older part of the subdivision in a cute little shell pink house. It was just big enough for one or two people, especially for a vacation home, and backed up to some woods. The front yard was tidy with one plastic pink flamingo in the flower bed and a sign out front that read *Singleton*. Beth pulled up in front and noticed the golf cart was still out. Just as she was wondering what the lot rent on a place that size was, Mrs. Singleton pulled into her driveway.

She hopped out of the golf cart and waved at Beth. "Good morning! Are you the detective?"

Beth waved back as she walked up the driveway. "Yes, I'm Detective Crandall. You must be Mrs. Singleton?"

"That's me. Come on in. Something cold sounds perfect right now. How about some iced tea?"

"Thank you. That would be nice."

A few minutes later, they were settled at the kitchen table. Mrs. Singleton had presented two tall iced teas in glasses with pink flamingos on them. She put little mats under each glass to catch the drips.

"All right, now. How can I be of help to you?"

Beth got out her notebook and pen. "You heard about the dead body in the lake over by the clubhouse, right?"

Gabby nodded. "I'm sure everyone in here has heard about that by now."

"And you heard the dead woman was the manager's wife, Rita?"

"Yes, I did hear that. I didn't see the body firsthand after they pulled it out of the lake, but I heard about it."

"Mrs. Singleton, the reason I asked to speak to you is that the initials GS were on Rita's phone, with your phone number and house number next to them."

"Please call me Gabby. Everyone does."

The detective smiled. "Okay, Mrs.sorry, Gabby. You can call me Beth if you'd like. Please tell me when you last saw or talked to her."

"Everyone saw her at that potluck. You couldn't miss her with a pea shooter."

"What do you mean?"

"I'm sure you heard how she was acting out worse than ever that night. I swear, the way Rita made a scene at most of those things made me think twice about going. I went anyway because I didn't want to let my friends down."

"Of course you didn't. So, you've seen her act like that before?"

"Look, I'm sure you've talked to other people who were there. Rita got drunk and picked on somebody at every single one of those clubhouse functions since she's been here, at least the ones I went to. I honestly don't know why she bothered going, unless she truly enjoyed making a scene. Maybe that was it...she enjoyed the attention, even bad attention."

Beth took a sip from her tea. "I've talked to several other people, but each person sees things that the others didn't. I'd like to know what you saw that night, if you don't mind."

Gabby slid her tea on its mat closer to her before she answered. "Sure, I'm happy to help in any way I can. That night, Rita made the rounds of the room as usual, saying obnoxious things to people—women in particular. She loved to pick on the older ladies for some reason. Before you laugh, by older I mean eighties or above. Anyway, until that night, she'd never sunk her claws into Edith."

"Really? That was the first time?" Beth made a note on her pad.

"As far as I know. At least that was the first time I saw her do it. Edith didn't come to every event at the clubhouse. She's almost ninety now and only has so much energy. She's a sweet thing, wouldn't hurt a fly."

"But Rita went after her anyway."

Gabby nodded, stabbing her finger in the air for emphasis on each of the first three words. "Yes, she did, making fun of the way Edith was dressed and all. I believe that's when Butch probably saw enough and hauled her off outside. That's what usually happened when Rita got out of control."

"So that was her usual behavior?"

"Oh, yes. We were all sick of it."

"And where were you sitting when this happened?"

"I was in my usual spot. My favorite table is toward the back of the room, and I was sitting there with several ladies I play golf with. I can give you their names if you'd like to talk to them, too. I'm sure everyone there would give you the same tale as to what Rita did that night."

Beth wrote something in her notebook before looking back up. "What else happened after that? Did you see Rita come back in?"

Gabby picked up her iced tea glass and took a sip. "Oh no, she never came back into the clubhouse. When Butch came back in without her, Rita's friend Kathy went out for a few minutes—I assume it was to talk to her—and then came back in. I didn't see Rita in the clubhouse again while I was there."

"Did you stay after that? Or did you go home?"

"Oh, I went home. I figured that was enough excitement for one evening."

"I can imagine. Now, back to my original question. Do you have any idea why Rita might've had your phone number and house number in her phone contacts?"

Gabby shrugged. "No clue whatsoever. I didn't think she even knew I lived here. We haven't spoken since she moved in. We had no reason to." Gabby sat back in her chair and crossed her arms, her head held high. "We don't travel in the same circle of friends you see, and she's definitely not my kind of person."

Beth nodded and made a couple more notes in her book. "Well, I do thank you for your time and for the information."

"No problem." Gabby uncrossed her arms as she smiled and leaned forward, her arms on the table. "I do have a couple of questions for you, if you don't mind."

Beth smiled back. "I'm happy to answer anything I can, if it's something I can release."

Gabby smiled back sweetly. "Like a lot of people in here, I'm sure, I'm curious about something. How did Rita's leg happen to wind up in Edith's yard? I mean, that does seem like an odd coincidence."

"We think one of the alligators bit it off and dragged it over there. Why it ended up in Edith's yard in particular, we have no idea."

Gabby looked at her iced tea for a few seconds. "Since you're asking so many questions around, I'm guessing the alligator didn't actually kill her?"

Beth shook her head. "No, we don't think so. It appears now like something else happened that landed Rita in the lake. Our working theory is that the alligator came along after she was already dead. It probably thought it would get an easy snack. It happened to carry what it took over to the lake behind Edith's house to munch on. Coincidence, probably."

"Good. I mean...well, I don't mean that it's good the leg wound up in Edith's yard. I meant it sounds like the local gators have been exonerated. That's good. Can't blame an alligator for trying to get a snack."

Beth smiled at her. "No, and the alligator didn't actually do anything but bite the leg off and carry it around. It looks like some human may have killed her."

Gabby appeared to have something else to say but appeared to think better of it.

"Is there something else you'd like to ask?"

"Well, I guess...I wonder if you're looking at anyone specific as a suspect. You probably can't tell me that."

"No, we can't. Rest assured we're looking at all the leads we get. If you have any information that might help us, please tell me."

"I don't think I know anything helpful. I'm being extra nosey, that's all. With so many rumors going around in here—I bet you've heard about some of them—this whole thing is driving us crazy."

"I'm sure. We're doing the best we can to get this solved as quickly as possible. Besides, her husband deserves to find out who killed his wife. Once we find out who, we can figure out why."

"Well, I doubt this will be news to you, but lots of people who live here would've loved to see her out of here, one way or another. To be honest, I don't think anyone other than Butch mourns her loss."

Beth tried not to chuckle, but she couldn't completely stifle it. "So I've heard."

Gabby reached over and patted Beth's hand. "Don't feel bad. I see you've talked to several of the residents here. I doubt anyone honestly liked her other than Butch. I don't think her friends did either, if they had to swear to it. Of course, I do feel sorry for poor Edith having to find that leg by the lake. That had to be quite a scare. I went over to her house as soon as I heard."

"Are you two close?"

"No, I wouldn't say that. We're just acquaintances. Well, close acquaintances, I guess you could say. I'm quite good at comforting people so I try to go over if I hear about anyone that needs some help."

"I see. And how did you hear about all of this?"

"Actually, it was Jess. She has a yard service and does my yard and Edith's, along with quite a few others in here. I asked her what was going on over at Edith's and she told me. I guess she was close by when Edith found the leg." Gabby took a little sip from her tea. "You know, Jess is a dear, always willing to help someone. She's also a retired police officer. Or maybe you already know that."

Beth smiled. "Yes, she told me when I interviewed her." She looked down at her notebook, pen in hand. "So...you went over to see Edith the day it happened?"

"Right. I wasn't there long, maybe thirty minutes. She seemed quite worn out by all the hullabaloo. I've been by a couple of times to check on her since then. She's such a nice woman and seems to be slowly getting over this. As I said, it's really too bad it had to happen to her."

Beth nodded. "Yes, it is. Anyway, if you think of anything else that might be of assistance, please call me." She handed Gabby her card. "We can use all the help we can get."

Chapter Twenty-two

JESS HAD JUST GOTTEN home when her phone went off. It was Beth. "Do you have some time to chat?"

"I can always make time for you. We can talk now if you want to talk on the phone. If you'd like to chat in person, I'm good with that too, if you give me a few minutes to get cleaned up. Want to come over in about an hour? I'll give you my gate code if you want."

She laughed. "Are you sure? Wow, I guess I've moved up in the world. Thanks, it would make it easier now that I know the way to your house."

Jess snickered. "I'm sure. I think I know you well enough now to rule out psycho ax murderer as your alter ego. It's 3197. See you in an hour."

Exactly an hour later, Beth pulled into Jess' driveway as Jess waved to her from the porch. In a few minutes more, they were settled into the cushions of her wicker chairs with iced tea glasses on the table between them.

Jess took a deep breath. "Hmm...the way you look right now, I'm guessing this isn't entirely a social call."

"You're right. Well, it's partly social since I do like to sit out here with you. I'd like for you to tell me what you know about Gabby Singleton."

That made Jess sit up straighter. "Gabby? Why? Is she a suspect?"

"I don't know yet. We found her initials, phone number, and house number in Rita's contact list."

"That's surprising. I didn't think they knew each other."

"Neither did I. I asked Butch if he knew why Gabby's info was in there and he had no idea, either. As far as he knew, they'd had no contact. He barely knew Gabby himself and only then because of the Leisure Lakes golf league. Rita played golf too, but according to Butch, she didn't join any of the community leagues. She insisted it was just a bunch of old people. She only played with members of her own little circle of friends."

"Okay, what would you like to know?"

"Do you remember when you told Gabby about Edith finding that leg?"

"I believe it was the same day it happened. Gabby always stopped me when she saw me, in case I'd heard something new I was willing to share. Most of the time, I don't pass on anything I hear, but she asks anyway. That morning, she'd seen some police cars and wondered what was going on. When I told her about the leg thing at Edith's, she said she was going straight over there to be of comfort. I understand she actually is good about showing up with food or other things for people who need them. Between you and me, I'm sure she also wants to see what is going on."

Beth nodded. "That's what she told me. I went to see her this morning and asked her about what she saw the night Rita was killed. Her account pretty much lined up with what I've heard from everyone else. She said she had no idea what her number was doing in Rita's phone since Rita never called her."

Jess grinned. "I'm surprised she didn't ask you who your main suspect was."

Beth grinned back. "She did, actually. Why?"

"Because she has to be the biggest busybody in the place. Don't get me wrong, she's a likeable busybody, but she loves knowing what's happening anywhere in Leisure Lakes. She has absolutely no filter when it comes to saying whatever comes to mind, usually. Everyone seems to like her just the same. I get a kick out of her, myself."

"Have you known her long?"

Jess picked up her tea and took a little sip. "I picked up her yard right after I started working at Leisure Lakes. Let's see, I'd say it was at least six years ago now. She's among the many that always come out to talk to me if they're home while I'm working there. She's quite a chatterbox, that one."

"Has she ever mentioned Rita before?"

"Not that I can think of. I never got the impression they had anything to do with each other. Ah...the phone number and house number thing. Can't you pull up Rita's phone records and see if they called each other?"

"Already did that. Nothing except a short call a while ago on Rita's phone record. It was so short I'm guessing she got voice mail and hung up. At this point, I guess she either didn't want to talk to an answering machine or realized it was a wrong number. Who knows? It was way too short for any conversation. The upshot is that Gabby said she never got a call from her."

Jess shrugged. "I doubt I know anything else really useful. Let's see. She's a widow. 'Her Harold,' as she always refers to him, died relatively young from a heart attack. She's never remarried. Oh, she did play softball when she was young, and she still carries a bat around with her in her golf bag. She says she's still got a good swing on her and she could fend off an alligator with it if she had to, like on the golf course or something. As I said, she's a nice woman who likes to gossip, like many others in here. Other than that," Jess looked up at the ceiling and back at Beth before shrugging again. "I can't think of anything."

Beth had been writing notes furiously. "That's good. At least I have a little more than I had before. I don't think she had anything to do with Rita's death, although my gut says she probably knows more than she's saying. Do you think the Leisure Lakes people would hide information about a murder? My overall impression is that no one liked Rita, and the general opinion of the ones I've interviewed is that Leisure Lakes is better off without her."

"Probably. Better off without her, I mean. I don't know if they'd go so far as to cover up for a killer. That's quite a leap."

Beth let out a sigh. "I know, but so far every lead has gone nowhere. The only oddball connection is this business with Gabby. I just can't imagine what that could mean."

"I'm sure it'll come to you, one way or another. My brain used to put things together while I was sleeping. I'd wake up in the middle of the night with an idea. It didn't always work out, but I always wrote down whatever the thought was. I'm sure by now you have your own way of coaxing ideas out."

"I do. I usually take a walk or clean the apartment whether it needs it or not. If that doesn't work, I go talk to a friend about something else. Sometimes ideas pop up on their own when I'm re-reading my notes for the fortieth time."

"Whatever you need to do to get your conscious mind off this and let it mush around in your subconscious, go for it. Is that why you came over today? Am I your distraction?"

Beth grinned. "You could say that. Well, there's something else I'd like to talk to you about."

"We're sitting here with a breeze and some iced tea. We can talk about anything you want, talk about nothing, or not talk at all if you'd like. It's nice to merely sit here."

Jess watched her iced tea glass sweat as the sounds of televised ball games drifted over from adjacent RVs. The aroma of someone grilling steaks down the street carried in on the breeze. They hadn't said much for several minutes, and Jess knew they were dancing around Beth's question. She decided to wait for Beth to say something first.

After a bit, Beth put her glass down. "Okay, here it is." She wiped the palms of her hands on her shorts. "There's something personal I'd like to talk to you about. Are you okay with that?"

"Personal. Fine. Shoot." Jess sat back in her chair, searching Beth's expression for what might be coming. It sounded...crap, she didn't know what it sounded like.

Beth smiled. "Don't worry, it's nothing awful. It's just that we haven't seen each other since we had dinner at my place. Did I do or say something wrong?"

Jess felt herself relax, and a little smile began to form at the edges of her lips. "I do like that you go straight to the point. You did nothing wrong. I've been busy, but..."

"But...?"

"It's been ages since someone other than my sister hugged me like you did. You seem like a touchy-feely person, at least with friends."

"Did it bother you?"

"It bothered me, but not in the way you think. I didn't want to take what you did the wrong way, and I decided it was best to leave it the way it was."

Beth bit her lower lip and smiled. "Jess, are you attracted to me at all?"

Jess felt her stomach clench. "Maybe. Sort of. Is this a trick question?"

"Here's the deal. I'm attracted to you. In fact, I like you a lot. Does that surprise you?"

"Yes, in a way. I've made no assumptions about you, other than you're a fun person and could be a good friend."

"You didn't get any vibes from me at all? I tried to send you some clues, but I didn't want to be too obvious."

Jess shook her head slowly, the little smile making its way from her lips to her eyes. "Nope. I wasn't looking, or at least I was trying not to."

Beth let out a sigh. "I know. Neither of us is looking for another partner right now. After this case is over I'd like to see if our friendship could be more than lunches and work talk. If you're interested, that is."

Jess looked into Beth's eyes and reached for Beth's hand. "I am. I've been interested since I first saw you, even though I've tried to ignore it. Remember, I warned you that I've had nothing but bad luck with relationships."

Beth smiled. "I'm a big girl. How about keeping it light for now? We have a lot in common and we enjoy each other's company. We could see if that's all there is or if there could be more down the road. If it turns out what we have now is all there is, that's okay with me. I don't want to lose you as a friend."

"That sounds like an excellent plan. I wouldn't want to lose you as a friend, either. At least now our feelings on both sides are out in the open." Jess smiled. "We can both relax. Well, I can relax around you now. Let's call us good friends right now. How's that?"

Beth put her other hand over Jess' hand. "Good friends. I like that."

Chapter Twenty-three

THE NEXT MORNING, BETH called Butch for an appointment, saying she needed a little more information about his wife. He said he'd be happy to see her at his office at nine-thirty for coffee and a chat. Right on time, he came out to the lobby and led her back to his office, where he had a carafe of coffee and two mugs ready for them. Once again, Beth noted how pleasant his office was.

Butch smiled and waved his hand across the room. "This was all decorated by the corporate office. They've worked hard to figure out what makes a great impression on buyers, and they set up each office themselves. I'm not allowed to turn my desk around, for instance, to look out that window behind me. The only time I get to enjoy that view is when I sit over here next to a visitor, like today. It's lovely, isn't it?"

"They do know how to make someone feel comfortable. Sitting here again, looking out that window is almost enough to make me want to live here." Beth smiled and put her Leisure Lakes logoed coffee mug down. "Again, almost."

Butch smiled and lifted his mug in a salute. "We'll have to keep working on you, then. We'd love to have you and I'm sure you'd enjoy living out here."

She reached into her jacket pocket for her notebook and pen. "You never know. I guess I could change my mind one of these days. Right now, I'm looking for a little more information about Rita, if you don't mind."

He put his mug down and regarded her. "No problem. I don't know what else I can tell you, but fire away."

"Let's start with this: What do you know about Rita's first marriage?"

Butch tilted his head to the side a little as he seemed to consider her question. He reached for his cup and took a sip "I never knew Rita's first husband. He'd been deceased for a few years when I met her. I did get the impression from things she told me that he wasn't particularly nice."

"What was Rita's last name when you met?"

"She'd taken back her birth name by then and was going by Rita

Lane. She said she didn't want any connection to her former husband. I know I once heard her husband's full name. It was Carl something. Unfortunately I don't remember his last name, since I never thought I'd need that information for anything. Is that important?"

"It might be. Remember I asked you if Rita knew Gabby Singleton?"

"Yes, I remember that. I still don't think their paths ever crossed here. I'm sure they didn't know each other."

"I'm still trying to figure out why Gabby's initials, phone number, and house number were in Rita's phone."

"Did you talk to Gabby?"

"I did. She said they weren't even acquaintances, and they never talked to each other. She didn't think Rita even knew who she was."

"Hmm...that sounds about right. They would've had nothing in common but golf, as far as I know. Since Rita didn't play in any of the ladies' leagues, they wouldn't have had any personal contact except passing each other in the clubhouse. The only other place they could've run into each other was the community potlucks. I've seen Gabby there, too."

Beth looked back down at her notebook. She wrote down a couple of things, and then looked back up at Butch. She held up her pen. "Do you think it's possible that Rita saw Gabby somewhere, like in the clubhouse or on the golf course, and she might've reminded her of someone?"

"I guess anything's possible. I don't know any of her old friends from back then except for Kathy. Rita told me both her parents were deceased, and I never met any of the rest of Rita's family, if there was any. She didn't stay in touch with any of her former husband's family, either. Rita told me she and Carl never had children. Maybe you should ask Kathy."

Chapter Twenty-four

WHEN BETH CALLED KATHY a little later, Kathy was just leaving to play golf. She said she didn't have time to talk and didn't want to miss her tee time.

"I'm sorry to bother you again, and I promise this will only take a minute or so. I have a couple of questions Butch said you might be able to answer."

Beth could hear Kathy's sigh on the other end. "Okay, I'll talk to you on the way there. Hold on a minute."

Beth heard the clunk sound of Kathy's golf cart brake releasing and the whine of the electric motor as she backed out of the driveway and started down the street. A few seconds later, Kathy said, "Go ahead, I'm ready." It sounded like she would love to have said something like 'this is a huge inconvenience' and 'get it over with fast.'

"Thanks for talking to me. Do you remember what Rita's former husband's name was?"

"Carl."

"Carl..."

"Oh, you want his last name. Singleton."

Beth felt her heartbeat speed up. "Did Carl have any siblings?"

"Just his brother Hal. His full name was Harold, if I remember correctly. He died ages ago, a long time before Carl did."

"Was Harold married?"

"I believe so, but I couldn't swear to it either way. I never met the brother or his wife if he was married. The Singleton brothers didn't have much to do with each other, apparently due to some kind of family feud they didn't talk about." She let out a sigh. "Okay, now that I think about it, I may have heard a wife mentioned once or twice. If I did hear of her, I can't remember her name now. That was decades ago. Listen, I'm at the clubhouse and I need to get going. Is there anything else you need?"

"I'm sorry. I need one more thing. Where did Carl die?"

"By then, they had moved to Westfield, New Jersey. Carl had an office there and in Manhattan, too. Now, is that all?" The impatience was quite evident in Kathy's voice now.

"Yes, thanks. I do appreciate your—" Beth heard a silence that told her Kathy cut off the call before Beth got past 'appreciate.' Beth took a deep breath. That was quite a change in attitude since their last chat. Even Rita's best friend was more involved with golf than worried about finding her best friend's killer. That seemed so sad, even for someone like Rita.

Chapter Twenty-five

BETH'S HANDS FLEW OVER the computer keyboard as she Googled Carl Singleton in Westfield, New Jersey. Since he and his wife were wealthy, they should've shown up in the society pages and the local paper should've given him a splashy death announcement. Even if it was fifteen or twenty years ago, there should be something searchable. If not, she could always find the local paper online and call them.

After a few minutes and several false starts, she found what she was looking for. The local paper had an obituary notice showing a photo of Carl Singleton, a dashing looking middle-aged man in a suit and tie. The picture looked like a professional headshot for a corporate website or brochure. The announcement mentioned that he'd passed away suddenly of heart failure. Listed among his family were his wife, Rita Singleton, and his predeceased parents by name. It also listed a predeceased brother, with no name listed. No sister-in-law or other grieving family members were mentioned.

Shoot, she thought. *That was some family not to even put the deceased brother's name in the obituary. How sad to think people could be that way, even after someone died.* She shook her head and slumped back in her chair.

She truly didn't want to think that Gabby Singleton could've killed someone. She seemed like such a likeable woman, so different from the now-dead Rita. If Rita had been Gabby's sister-in-law, what could've made Gabby mad enough to do something drastic after all this time?

Harold had died quite a while before Carl, but she tried checking the same city's newspaper for older obits with Harold's name anyway, since they were the only newspaper in the county. She gave up after half an hour of searching. It was apparently too old. She ended up calling the newspaper for the information that would've been in their microfiche or other old files at least. They found it and read it to her over the phone. There it was. Harold Singleton left behind a grieving widow named Gabriella Singleton. It had to be the same Gabby. She had them send the information to her office email.

She hated to have to do it, but it was time to talk to Gabby again, this time as a possible suspect. She sincerely hoped she was wrong and decided it was best to ask to see her at her home. If she was wrong about her, it would be easy to back out of the interview and let it go. She called Gabby and set up a meeting for the next morning. She was sure she was putting it off because she wasn't looking forward to it, but she was equally sure Gabby wasn't going anywhere.

Her first inclination was to call Jess and lay all this out in front of her to get her own head straight. It wouldn't hurt to get her opinion before she got into it with Gabby, but she probably shouldn't. Or maybe she should. Jess was the only person she knew who also knew Gabby.

She punched in Jess' phone number.

"Hi Beth! What's up?" Jess' voice was happy and cheerful sounding. Beth knew that would change.

Beth's voice was neither happy nor cheerful. "I have something on this case I need to talk to you about. In private. Your place or mine?"

"Either. Which one are you closer to?"

"Mine it is. Can you meet me there in, say, half an hour?"

"Sure. Are you okay?"

"I'm not sure right now. When you see what I'm going to show you, you probably won't be, either. See you in a bit."

***

Twenty-five minutes later, Jess walked up to Beth's door as she was unlocking it. Beth had a bag with her and a folder under her arm.

"Am I glad to see you!" Beth pushed the door open. After tossing her bag and the file on the table and shutting the door behind them, she threw her arms around Jess. "I so need a hug," she said against Jess' shoulder.

"Of course you can have a hug." Jess pulled Beth closer and held her. After a short bit, she felt Beth relax. Jess put her hands on Beth's shoulders and leaned back to see her face. Looking her in the eyes, she could see that Beth was shaken up about something. "Let's sit down and talk this out. Whatever's bothering you, we'll try to come up with a solution."

"Thank you." Beth led the way to the living room and sat on the couch. "I feel kind of silly letting this case get to me. I'm an experienced detective and I should've built up thicker skin. When you see what I have you'll understand."

"All right, I'm ready. Let's hear it. I'm a good listener...really, I am." Jess smiled.

Beth shook her head. "You aren't going to like this."

Jess put her hands up. "What? Oh, no, are you going to put George down after all? A lot of people out there at Leisure Lakes would be up in arms."

Beth shook her head again, putting one of her hands up in the stop position. "No, no, no. Your beloved alligator's safe." She reached for Jess' hand, staring at it as in contemplation. She tightened her grip as she looked up into her eyes. "It's Gabby."

Jess jerked her hand away. "Gabby? What does Gabby have to do with any of this? I know she was at that potluck when all the action happened. She's pretty much at all of them, mostly so she won't miss any gossip if you ask me. She went over to be with Edith the day the leg showed up in her yard, but I told her about that."

Beth took a deep breath and looked at the ceiling for a moment, appearing to contemplate her next words, then she blurted it out. "It's possible Gabby had something to do with Rita's death."

Jess' stomach clenched and she closed her eyes for a few seconds as if to shut out what she heard Beth say. "Gabby? No…I can't imagine that. She's a busybody, yes, and quite a character, too. I can't see her as a murderer." She stared at Beth. "Are you sure?"

Beth shook her head. "No, I'm not absolutely sure. If I was, I would've arrested her already. The evidence, however, is heading more and more in that direction. I hate to think that someone as nasty as Rita got away with all kinds of misery-causing stuff, and someone who seems as nice as Gabby could be her murderer."

"Okay, show me what you have, and let's see what led you down this road."

Beth went to the table and retrieved the folder. She spent the next twenty minutes laying out what she'd been researching and what the results had been. "I can't even imagine how awful it must've been for Gabby and her husband to be related to Rita and her first husband. For Rita to deliberately leave Harold's name out of Carl's obituary—that was horrible. There must've been quite some bad blood between them."

Jess kept staring at some of the printouts Beth had spread out on the table. "You know, Gabby has been a widow for decades now. Rita and Butch have been living at Leisure Lakes for several years and nothing happened between Gabby and Rita. As far as we know, there's been no interaction at all between them. That's a long time for someone to carry any kind of grudge, and besides, Gabby doesn't seem like the grudge-carrying sort. She always seems so happy."

"That's what I've seen and heard about her, too. I can't imagine what could've tipped her over the edge to do something to Rita. I'm going to interview her again tomorrow. No way around it. She didn't tell me that Rita was her sister-in-law, information pertinent to the case—or could be. I could call that withholding evidence if I wanted to be a stickler about it."

"True, but she's technically a former sister-in-law. Rita's previous husband, the one related to Gabby's husband, is long dead, and Rita has remarried. Plus, it's been ages since all that happened, and—"

Beth held her hand up. "Okay, I get it. All right. If nothing else comes of this, I won't hit her with withholding evidence charges. I'm hoping that mentioning possible charges might be enough to open up. The big thing here is, do I genuinely want to know?"

"And the answer to that is...?"

"I don't. If this wasn't a murder, I'd try to figure out a way to keep her out of this if I could. But I can't."

"No, you can't." Jess shook her head slowly as she spoke. "As much as you might like her and dislike the victim, of course you can't."

"I can't ignore what I found out and I do have to talk to her again. See, you do understand, and you throw reality right back at me...in a good way, of course."

"I try. Look, you already knew what you had to do, even if you weren't looking forward to it. You just wanted someone else who's been there to remind you of it. That's what friends are for." Jess smiled at her.

Beth smiled back. "You're right all around. If you hadn't been a detective yourself, I would never have talked to you about any of this. I know it's safe to talk to you, to bounce things off you, knowing this goes nowhere else. You have no idea how good that feels."

"Don't you have a work partner? I've never seen you out at Leisure Lakes with another detective, but I never thought much about it until now."

Beth sighed. "No. That's not how it works here. This is a relatively minor case, even though it's a murder investigation. I'm afraid I got it because I'm the low man—or woman, in this case—on the totem pole. The other detectives already had several cases assigned to them, and I had just finished up my last one. That meant I got it. Plus, I'm sure they thought it'd be cute to give me an alligator case. I don't think anyone believed this thing would drag on so long. I was supposed to simply make sure it was an alligator that took her leg off, figure out which one did it, then call animal control to have it dragged away. End of case. Move on to the next one. Kind of an initiation into Florida life." She looked away, her gaze unfocused. "Regrettably, it hasn't turned out like that."

"No, it hasn't," Jess said. "But if there's a positive thing about this whole situation, it's that we met. I'm glad we did."

"So am I. It helps to have someone in your life that understands what you're going through, that's for sure."

Jess reached her arm around Beth's shoulders. "It does. Good friends can be hard to come by."

Chapter Twenty-six

PROMPTLY AT NINE THE next morning, Beth knocked on Gabby's front door. Gabby appeared at the door so fast Beth assumed she'd been standing there waiting for her. After the 'good mornings' and other pleasantries, they sat at the kitchen table once more.

Beth smiled at her as she took out her notebook and pen. "Gabby, I know you're wondering why I needed to come back and talk to you again."

Gabby smiled back, crossing her arms over her chest. "I'm not completely surprised. You found out Rita used to be my sister-in-law, didn't you?"

"Yes, I did."

"All right. I should've told you, I guess. That was a lifetime ago, and I certainly don't claim her as a relative."

"You should've told me anyway, no matter how long ago it was."

Gabby leaned back in her chair. "First of all, it was a mercy killing."

This got raised eyebrows and pursed lips from Beth. "Mercy killing? What are you talking about?"

Gabby put her hands up. "I killed Rita. I assume that's where you're headed with all of this."

Beth felt her stomach clench. "Are you actually telling me you had something to do with her death?"

Gabby continued to smile at her. "Yes, I did. I killed her."

"Okay, before we go any farther, I need to read you your rights." She read the Miranda rights card to her and reminded her, "You don't have to say anything else to me without an attorney present, you know."

"I know, and I want to tell you what happened. Rita was a miserable woman, and she had reason to be. When her first husband was gone, I'm sure she realized it was too easy to do away with someone. She got away with it. Don't you see? Even after all these years, she still had to live with what happened."

"What do you think she did, Gabby?"

"Rita figured out a way to murder her first husband to get all his money, instead of divorcing him like most women would."

"Excuse me? Are you saying Rita was a murderer?"

Another little smile teased at the corners of Gabby's mouth, accompanied by a tilt of her head. "That's exactly what I'm saying, even though I've never been able to prove it."

Beth raised her eyebrows again, looked down, and wrote something on her notepad before looking back at Gabby. "All right. Go on."

"I'm sure it just about killed her to carry on the grieving widow act as long as she did when all she wanted was to do the happy dance after getting away with it. From then on, she had to act like someone she wasn't. She thought she'd be happy with Carl gone, but I know she wasn't. A woman like Rita needs a man in her life."

"Lots of women do, you know."

"Rita needed more than that. She needed to dress in the most current clothes and parade around on a good-looking man's arm. That, at least, she got from Carl. On the other hand, she also craved love and attention from that same man."

"Which she didn't get, I assume?"

"No, I don't think she did, especially toward the end. When she met Butch, I'm sure she thought she'd be happy again. He does seem like a nice guy and I'm sure they must've been happy for a while. He gave her the love and attention she craved, but he isn't into the showy material things. He seems to be a much more down-to-earth kind of guy. When he took this job and moved her to a retirement community, there she was again, unhappy and wanting out. She should've divorced him and moved on to the next guy. Instead, there was just enough incentive to keep her from doing anything rash. Unfortunately, there wasn't enough to keep her from making those around her miserable."

"So, what did you do?"

"That night after Rita made the big scene in the clubhouse, I saw Butch take Rita outside to calm her down. A short while later, he came back in without her. I knew she had to be somewhere on the lawn or on the dock, drunk, but at least she wasn't bothering anyone. Kathy stopped Butch to say something to him. When she went outside, I assumed it was to sit with Rita. I decided to go outside myself and smoke a cigarette about then, so I could see what was going on."

"Do you think Kathy saw you?"

"No. I know she didn't since she never looked in my direction. By then, it was nearly dark, and it was easy to stay in the shadows. You probably noticed there are woods on either side of the clubhouse, and I took the door leading out the left side while she went out the right side. Look, I know smoking's a nasty habit and I try not to smoke anywhere near anyone else when I must have one." She looked up dramatically and shook her head. "My dear departed husband, Harold, hated that I smoked, but he put up with it as long as I did it outside."

"Gabby, can we move on with your story? What did you see out there?"

"Oh, yes. Of course. Anyway, after that scene she'd made in the clubhouse, picking on poor Edith like she did, I knew Rita had probably reached the boiling over point and was headed for big trouble again." She sighed dramatically. "I actually felt sorry for Rita, you know. She was such a miserable creature."

"Gabby..."

She shook her head hard as if shaking the cobwebs away. "Sorry. Anyway, I heard Rita go after her friend Kathy, who had never been anything but supportive for so long. My, my...what she put up with. That's a good friend for sure. When I heard that, I knew I'd seen enough. I put out my cigarette and waited for Kathy to go back into the clubhouse. I walked down to have it out with Rita myself. Enough was enough of that nonsense. Her misery was her own doing."

"Then what?"

"I walked out to the pier, sat down next to Rita, and quietly told her exactly who I was, what I knew about her, and that either she was going to stop what she was doing to everyone or I was going to tell what I knew."

"Was she surprised to see you? I mean, you said you hadn't had any contact with her."

"I guess so. She did sit there and stare at me for a few seconds before she started laughing. What she said next was, 'You wouldn't dare. No one will ever believe you.' I remember that clearly. It was the laughing part that finally did it. It was possible no one would believe me since I have no real proof. That was when I decided to walk away and let her do whatever she did, since I couldn't stop her legally. I remember I stood up and walked out to my golf cart."

Beth stared at her. "So, you left her there? How did you kill her if you left?"

"I was going to leave. I didn't. By the time I got out to the parking lot, I knew I just couldn't let her keep hurting people like she did. I reached into the back of my golf cart and got the old baseball bat I kept in case of alligators on the golf course. I remember it felt good in my hands and I knew what I needed to do. I thought maybe if she knew I could hurt her, she'd back off. Most bullies, you know, are cowards. At that point, I only planned to give her a good scare."

"How long were you gone?"

"I don't know, several minutes. Long enough to walk around the clubhouse to my golf cart and take time to think about what I was going to do."

"Could it have been as long as ten minutes?"

"Possibly, or a bit longer. I walked back down to the pier with the bat in my hand. She was still alone, and I confronted her again. This time she looked like she'd been drenched with a bucket. As drunk as she was, she must've fallen off the dock and gotten back out of the water. She stood up and held her hands out in the universal 'bring it on' gesture." Gabby stood up and demonstrated. "She shouldn't have done that. I swung that bat around like I was hitting a home run and her head was the softball. I remember hearing the wood contacting her head and it and the rest of her going over the side of the pier into the water. Afterward, I threw that bat as far out into the lake as I could, walked back to my golf cart, and left."

"You didn't see Kathy pushing her into the water then?"

"Oh, no, she just pushed her down onto the bench as far as I could tell. Rita wasn't wet when I first came out, but she was when I came back the second time. I've no idea how that happened. No matter. I was the one who knocked her into the water for good."

"Are you sure?"

"I'm sure. Look, I never liked Rita, but until she came here she was just a self-centered rich girl. My dear departed Harold and Rita's first husband Carl were brothers, but as different as night and day. My Harold was ten years older than Carl. Where my Harold was a sweetheart, Carl was a spoiled brat who became an up-and-comer whose only mission in life seemed to be making a lot of money before he was forty. And he did. He married Rita because she was great arm candy, as they say nowadays. They had the house and the fancy parties and all that stuff that we didn't. In fact, the only time Carl paid much attention to Rita was when he needed her on his arm for some event with press pictures. When he wanted her for something, it was the whole 'perfect couple' thing with the mile-wide smiles that showed up in the society columns."

Beth shook her head. "That's too bad. And they never had any children?"

Gabby sighed. "It was too bad. And no, they never had children. Oddly enough, I felt sorry for her in a way, even then. She married him for what he could give her, but whatever he gave her was never going to be enough. Not enough love. Not enough attention. He did throw money at her for anything she wanted and expected her to be happy with that. Even though I don't know exactly how she did it, I'm sure she killed him somehow or had him killed. You can tell when someone's walking around with something eating at them, even though it got her what she wanted."

"But didn't she know you lived here? I mean, you are sort of relatives. Or were, anyway. Why do you think she put your phone number and house number in her phone, with your initials?"

"I have no idea. She never called me that I can recall. At least, we never spoke. She never came to my house; I know that for sure. We didn't have much to do with each other even when we were sisters-in-law all those years ago. After my Harold passed on, there was no reason for them to have anything at all to do with me. Simply out of some strange curiosity, I did follow their goings-on in the society pages for a while after I became a widow, knowing what a crock their social act was. I didn't say anything to anyone about them, and I completely dropped off their radar." She lifted her shoulders in a slight shrug. "That was fine by me. By the time Rita and Butch moved here, it had been decades since my Harold passed away. I kept my married name, but it's a fairly common one. I'm sure she didn't know I was here for quite a while, if ever. That's why I'm surprised she had my number, unless she randomly found it in the Leisure Lakes directory. Anyway, it's been so long that I was sure she wouldn't recognize me, even passing in the clubhouse, with my grey hair and all. She never spoke to me or picked on me at any of those gatherings, and I left her alone. Until that night."

"You could've walked away and lived the rest of your life without confessing. Why did you decide to tell me all of this?"

"Because, unlike some people, I couldn't let you keep investigating other possible suspects and let the whole Dead Rita thing go on forever. You might've decided to charge someone else with it. I'm only sorry the gators didn't want to finish Rita off after all." She laughed. "I guess even they didn't like the taste of her."

Beth's phone rang, and without looking, she let it go to voicemail. It immediately rang again. It was her office.

"Hold on, I need to take this. Don't go anywhere."

Gabby laughed as Beth answered her phone. Quietly, she said, "I have no plans at the moment."

Beth answered the phone. "Crandall here."

The voice on the other end said, "You need to get down here immediately. You'll never believe what's happening."

"I'm in the middle of something right now. Give me a clue why I need to drop what I'm doing."

"Three people are here to confess to killing your victim."

"What?"

"You heard it. Three."

Beth ended the call. "Gabby, you must come with me to the station. It appears you have some competition for the title of Rita's killer."

Gabby held her hands out as if for handcuffs.

Beth shook her head. "I don't think you'll need them. Go get your handbag if you'd like, and I'll search it before we leave. After that, you're good to go."

Chapter Twenty-seven

BETH WALKED INTO HER office with Gabby in tow and was surprised to see several elderly people, some she recognized from Leisure Lakes, sitting in chairs against the wall. They each had bottles of water, and they seemed to be chatting among themselves as if this was a social occasion. That seemed odd to Beth. They didn't usually let suspects talk to each other like that. She assumed it was because no one believed them. As she passed the group, they all waved and said hi to Gabby. Beth watched Gabby wave back as they continued past them. She put Gabby in a chair next to her desk and, after getting her a bottle of water, asked her to stay there.

The detective at the next desk started chuckling, followed by, "Either you've got nobody, or you have the whole place confessing. Good luck with that."

Beth gave him a fake smile that was a cross between 'thanks' and 'screw you.' "Has anyone actually talked to these people?"

"Nope, they asked to see you. By name. And three of them told us they were the one that killed your victim. We thought we should save them all for you."

Beth sighed. "Oh, goody." She walked back over to the little group, who seemed to be having quite a good time chatting among themselves. She stood there for a bit before they noticed her. "Okay now, I was told some of you came in here to confess to killing Rita Grayson. Is that right?"

Three heads nodded enthusiastically.

Beth rolled her eyes inwardly but outwardly smiled at them. "All right, who wants to go first?"

Three hands went up. She pointed at the gentleman on the end and motioned for him to follow her.

Chapter Twenty-eight

"MR. HANCOCK, I UNDERSTAND you want to confess to killing Rita Grayson. Is that correct?"

Kevin Hancock appeared to be about eighty, a tall, slender man with sun-dried wrinkles on his face and arms. Beth guessed they were from playing golf. He adjusted his Leisure Lake logoed baseball cap and nodded. "Yes, ma'am. I did it."

Beth nodded. "All right then, first I'll read you your rights and if you still want to talk to me, we'll hear how you did it and why."

A minute later, after being Mirandized and saying he understood his rights, Mr. Hancock sat back in his chair with his arms crossed and continued. "Well..." — his drawl pulling that word into several syllables—"I can imagine you've talked to enough people at Leisure Lakes to know how nearly everyone hated Rita. She was a mean, nasty woman who was rude every time I saw her. The last straw was when she decided to mess with Edith. Edith is such a sweet lady that I can't imagine anyone wanting to hurt her, but that's exactly what Rita did that night at the clubhouse."

"I've pretty much heard that from everyone I've talked to. Please tell me your tale of what happened that night."

Kevin leaned forward, his arms on the table. "To tell you the truth, we were all pretty much fed up with her even before she tore into poor Edith. I tend bar at the 19th Hole at the main golf course. If we work enough hours for the park, we get free golf. Anyway, Rita never had a pleasant word to say to anyone, except maybe that little crew she hung out with. She was such a vicious woman, I kept expecting her to snarl like a wild cat every time I saw her. That night at the clubhouse, everyone brought in their own beverages, including liquor. They each had their names on their bottles, but I was mixing the alcoholic drinks. When Rita came for hers that night, I put mostly alcohol in hers, hoping she'd get so drunk she'd pass out and go home early."

"So, you're the one responsible for her being even drunker than usual that night."

"Yes, that was my fault. It backfired completely. Her tolerance turned out to be much higher than I suspected and it just made her meaner, quicker. So, you see, she's dead because of me. If I hadn't done that, she might not have been out on the pier and Butch might've taken her home. Whatever happened after that was my fault."

"Mr. Hancock—" Beth tried to interrupt him.

"No, really. I wanted her dead or at least gone. If I could've slipped her something more, I would've. I watch those mysteries on TV and believe me, if I thought I could've bought something and slipped it into her drink to get rid of her, I would've. Good riddance to bad rubbish, I say. Butch is better off without her and so is the entire place. All of Leisure Lakes can agree on that, at least."

"Mr. Hancock—" she tried again.

He put his wrists together as if they were already shackled. "Handcuff me now and take me away. Everyone else can go home. My wife just came with me and didn't have anything to do with it, either."

"That's nice of you, but I don't think they can go home quite yet. I'm going to need to hear all their stories now, too."

"I'm trying to save you some work here. Gabby is no murderer. I can see you have her in your sights, but I know she didn't kill Rita. If Rita hadn't been so drunk, she wouldn't have been out there."

"I understand. Please bear with me on this. When we're done here, I'd like you to sit in our breakroom away from the rest of your buddies out there. After I'm finished with the rest of them, we'll see what the complete story is, hopefully. Oh, and by the way, how did you find out I was bringing Gabby in?"

"She called some of us last night after you said you wanted to see her again. She wanted to make sure we didn't get mad at her for what she did. She also wanted to be sure her place was taken care of while she was in jail and the golf schedules were taken care of. She's quite passionate about golf, you know."

"I can see that. Did she ask you to come down here?"

He put his hands up. "Oh, heck no. I'm sure she's shocked to see us."

"Did you all come down here together?"

Kevin's eyebrows shot up. "Oh, no. I was surprised to see the rest of them. I'm sure they each came on their own, like I did."

Beth slid a legal pad and a pen across the table to him. "Mr. Hancock, I need you to write down what you told me on this pad, just like you explained it to me. When you're done, let us know and one of the detectives will take you to the breakroom. If you'd like, your wife can join you in there. Just tell the detective and he'll go get her."

Chapter Twenty-nine

THE NEXT TO BE interviewed was Irene Watson. Plopping herself into the indicated chair at the interview table, she proudly announced that she was Rita's killer. She dramatically adjusted her bra straps under the bright red knit top she wore. Afterward, being fully readjusted, she reached for her huge lime green handbag and held it up close to her like a baby. She reeked of cigarette smoke.

Beth tried not to cough, but she couldn't help herself. "Okay, Mrs. Watson, let me read you your rights. After I'm convinced you understand them, you can tell me whatever you want to tell me."

A minute or so later, fully Mirandized, Irene started back in again, her head held high. "I did it. You can send everyone else back home."

"Hmmm...I'm seeing a trend here. Are you sure you want to talk to me without your attorney?"

Irene nodded vigorously. "I want to get this off my chest. And please call me Irene."

"All right, Irene, what did you do?" Beth let out another little cough.

"I got rid of that nasty woman," she said, her head held high and shoulders straight. "She needed to go. No one—maybe except for Butch—will miss that witch with a B, that's for sure."

"All right, tell me exactly what happened."

"I saw Butch take Rita outside. Well, everybody did. When he came back in without her, I saw Kathy go out the same door. I assumed she went to sit with her. Kathy came back in a few minutes later, looking like she was about to cry. Obviously, Rita had gone after Kathy, too. I thought about it for a few minutes, then went outside myself. I didn't see anyone else but Rita sitting on the dock, so I went down there and yelled at her. I told Rita how awful she was acting and that she had no right to treat people like that. She stood up, even though she was a little wobbly, and started laughing. You know, that was very rude, too. When she laughed at me, I got even madder at her. I swung my purse around to hit her as hard as I could, and I knocked her down onto the dock. She looked like she was out cold, so I rolled her into the water, where I assume she drowned. I waited for a few seconds to make sure she wasn't coming back up, which she didn't."

"Did you hit her with the purse you're carrying now?"

"Yes, I always carry it. It's my favorite."

"Okay, after all that happened, did you go back into the clubhouse?"

"I did. I had to get my casserole dish. Even with my name on the bottom of it, it could've gotten misplaced or someone could've walked off with it. A good casserole dish is hard to come by, you know."

"I'm sure. What happened after that?"

Irene raised her eyebrows and sat up even straighter. "I went home, of course. Where else would I have gone?"

"Did you see anyone else near the dock while you were out there?"

"No, but I wasn't looking. I just hurried back up to the clubhouse."

Beth pushed a yellow legal pad and a pen across the table. "Okay, I need you to write down all of what you just told me. Can you do that?"

Irene smiled sweetly. "Yes, I can. Am I under arrest now?" She sounded almost eager to have the handcuffs slapped on.

"Not yet. When you're done, come on out and let me or one of the other detectives know, and we'll take you to the breakroom to wait until I've talked to all of you."

Beth closed the door behind her and coughed a few times before attempting some deep breaths. Her chest hurt just from the smell of smoke coming off Irene. She stopped by the detective's desk nearest the interview room Irene was in and asked him to please spray some air freshener in there when Irene came out. She went down the hall and grabbed a bottle of water from the fridge. A few swallows later, and she was ready for the next alleged killer.

Chapter Thirty

THE NEXT ONE TO request an interview was a surprise. Beth wasn't sure at first where she could recall him from, but before she could figure it out, the man reached out his hand and introduced himself.

"Hi, I'm Ed Blake. I'm Kathy's husband. You came to our house recently to talk to her about her friend, Rita."

Beth shook his hand. "Oh, yes, now I remember you." She motioned to the chair across the table. "Please sit down, Mr. Blake. Are you here to confess to killing Rita too?"

He nodded. "Yes, I am. No matter what the others said, I'm the one that killed her. And please call me Ed."

"Okay then, Mr...Ed. Let me read you your rights, and afterward you can decide what you still want to say to me without an attorney present."

A couple of minutes later, after Ed said he understood his rights, Beth asked him if he still wanted to talk to her without his attorney present. He clasped his hands together on the table in front of him as if already shackled. "I do. I want this over with."

"All right. First of all, I didn't see your wife out there. Does she know you're here?"

"No. She thinks I'm running errands. She doesn't know anything about this, and I didn't want her drawn into it any more than she had to be."

Beth reached into her pocket for her notebook and pen. She had to turn several pages to get to a blank one. "I understand. All right, Ed, what do you want to tell me about what happened the night Rita was killed?"

"Well, as you know, Rita got even drunker and meaner than usual at that party in the clubhouse. After she'd been around the room saying obnoxious things to people, she settled on Edith Bradshaw. The way she made fun of her was way, way out of line, even for Rita. Everybody knows Edith, and I'm sure they'd agree with me that she's a little ray of sunshine." He sighed. "Such a sweet woman. She's always smiling every time I've seen her."

Beth nodded. "I can imagine Rita picking on her would've made the others mad."

"It did. We thought she'd stop after a minute and she'd get bored and move on. That's what she usually did. Unfortunately, she kept at it this time. Edith started to cry, I'm sure because she was so embarrassed. Apparently, that made Rita go after her like a shark smelling blood. I hoped someone would intervene, but each time someone sitting by Edith started to do just that, Rita gave them dirty looks like they could be next. Then she'd up the Edith-bashing another level. By then, Butch must've heard what was happening and made a beeline to grab Rita. He grabbed her by the arm, made an apology to Edith, and took his struggling wife out the side door. It looked like he was talking to her under his breath the whole way out, trying to get her to settle down, but she was having none of it. She kept trying to get loose and we could hear her telling him to let her go. We figured she'd have some real bruises on her arm the next day from that. If she tried to say anything about abuse, though, he had all of us as witnesses to the contrary."

"That sounds pretty much like what everyone else has told me so far, Ed. What happened after that?"

He looked at the ceiling then down at his hands again. "Kathy and I were sitting there, stunned. We'd never seen Rita act out that badly before. She and Kathy were best friends, you know, and we'd seen Rita drunk and disorderly, but that was the worst we'd ever seen her. At that point, several people had gathered around Edith. Some hugged her and told her it'd be all right and she was just fine as she was. I heard someone tell her she shouldn't worry about anything Rita said. A few minutes later, Butch came back in. That's when Kathy went to ask him how Rita was doing. I tried to get her to stay out of it, but she insisted."

"Then what?"

"Kathy came back and said believe it or not, Butch hadn't taken Rita home. He'd just taken her out to sit on the dock. He told Kathy he thought the air and quiet outside might calm her down. That's when Kathy told me she was going to go sit with her. I asked her again to stay out of the whole situation, but she again insisted. She asked me, what kind of friend would she be if she abandoned her? I told her that with Rita, it was take, take, take. She didn't deserve Kathy's concern. Needless to say, she went anyway."

"How long was she gone?"

"I'm not sure. A bit. I know now that I should've gone with her or at least stood outside to keep an eye on them, but I didn't. By the time

Kathy came back in, her eyes were red, and she was nearly in tears, wanting to go home. I told her we should just stay, since the drama was all over, and we did stay for a few minutes more. Kathy was still quite upset and wanted to leave so much that we packed up our things and I took her home."

"All right, how did you manage to do away with Rita if you left?"

"When we got home, I almost immediately made an excuse to return to the clubhouse alone. I told her I dropped something and was going to go look for it. What I was planning to do was have it out with Rita if she was still around and tell her she was never going to step foot in our house again for any reason. Ever."

"You had a feeling she was going to make her way back to your place instead of going home that night?"

"Exactly. That was not—and I mean not—going to happen at all if I had to sit by the door and call 911 to keep her out. Anyway, by the time I got back, I saw Gabby out there with Rita. Rita looked like she'd gotten wet somehow. I assumed she'd fallen off the dock. Gabby had her baseball bat with her, and I could tell something awful was about to happen. I didn't care what happened to Rita, but I couldn't let that happen to Gabby. I ran down there and grabbed the bat from her. I told her to go home and I'd take care of things."

"Did she leave?"

"She left the dock, but she didn't want to leave. I told her to go home—now. And as far as I know, she did."

Beth made a couple of notes. "Then what?"

"Rita started laughing." He looked back up at Beth. "You know, she and I had a rotten relationship. It mostly amounted to me trying to order her out of our house. Kathy almost always took her side, saying that Rita didn't have any other friends to turn to. No place else to go. I always told Rita to go home and stop acting like this was her other house and we were her caretakers."

"I can guess that wasn't fun."

"No, it wasn't. Rita was the sole problem Kathy and I had in our marriage. I've never been able to figure out what in the world Kathy saw in Rita or why she wanted to stay friends with her after all that. I simply couldn't take it anymore. I couldn't let Kathy take it anymore. And I sure couldn't let Gabby kill her. I had come down to the lake to have it out with Rita myself, since she treated Kathy so badly, and after all Kathy did for her.

"As I stood there with the bat in my hand, I realized I wanted the pleasure of killing Rita for myself. Rita stood there laughing at me and taunting me, and I took that bat and swung for the fences with it. When I felt it contact her...it was her head, I think, I admit it felt good. I wasn't sorry at all that I'd done it. She went over the side into the water and didn't come up. I waited for a minute or so and figured she was tangled up in the grasses and the like below the dock. I didn't make any effort to get her out. None at all. I stood there and hoped she was gone for good."

"Did Gabby see you do this?"

"No, I don't think so. I'm sure she assumed it was me, though. Everyone knows Rita deserved what she got. I threw that bat as far as I could out into the lake, figuring that would keep it from ever being found."

"So, Gabby didn't kill her after all. I wonder why she admitted to it."

"You'd have to ask her. It's possible that since she didn't get her bat back, she assumed I went through with what she had planned to do herself. I don't know why she would confess to something she didn't do."

Beth had been watching him intently as he told his story. "What made you come in today to tell me this?"

"I heard through the grapevine that you talked to Gabby the other day. Kathy told me that you had asked her about Gabby, twice. I assumed it was only a matter of time before you came looking for me, if Gabby told you the truth about what happened. Then last night, I heard Gabby was making calls to arrange for someone else to handle the golf league and she loves that golf league. That's when I knew she was about to confess to something she didn't do. She wanted to do it, believe me, but I stopped her. I couldn't let that happen."

Beth closed her notebook and put her pen down. "I think you should know, Gabby never mentioned you at all. She had me convinced she'd killed Rita. She had the whole story, including throwing the bat in the lake, so she must've seen or heard you do it."

"It's possible." He looked at his hands. "She should've gone home when I told her to."

"I can only assume she knew just enough to assume you'd taken care of Rita. Now, I need you to write all that down for me." Beth passed him a legal pad and a pen. "Then you'll want to call your wife and your attorney, not necessarily in that order."

Chapter Thirty-one

JESS' PHONE WENT OFF just as she was finishing lunch. She glanced at it, smiling when she saw who it was.

"Hi Joni. What's up? Did you bake some more cookies?"

Her sister's voice sounded grave. "No. Are you sitting down?"

"I'm sitting on my tailgate in front of the Harvey's house. I just finished my lunch. What's wrong? Wait...are you okay? Do I need to come over there?" She jumped off the tailgate and started digging in her pocket for her keys.

"I knew you wouldn't have gotten any news today, so I thought I'd better tell you. The police have arrested someone for Rita's murder! It's on TV right now."

"What? Who? When? Oh, my God. I'll be there as fast as I can." She slammed the tailgate shut and sprinted to the cab of her truck.

Joni continued her story. "It's all over the local news. You'll never guess who they arrested, either."

Jess jumped into her truck, and as she turned the key in the ignition and put it in gear, she looked up at the heavens. *Please don't let it be Gabby, please don't let it be Gabby,* she thought, over and over. Her heart pounded as she pulled away from the curb. She practically yelled into the phone, "The suspense is killing me. Just tell me who it was!"

"It's Ed Blake, Kathy's husband."

Jess felt her world stand still for just a second, then she breathed a sigh of relief. Thank God, it wasn't Gabby after all.

"Jess? Are you there? You do their yard, don't you?"

"Yes, I'm here. I'm a couple of blocks away from your place now. I guess I'm just...wow...shocked, I guess. Be there in a minute."

Jess ended the call and shortly parked her pickup in front of Joni's house. She sat there for a good minute, trying to figure out what had happened. Sitting on Joni's steps, she untied her dirty boots and pulled them off before doing her special knock and letting herself into the house.

Joni pointed to the sheet she had thrown over one of the chairs so Jess could sit and see the TV. On the side table was a glass of iced tea waiting for her on its coaster. "I still can't believe it."

"I can't either," Jess said as she picked up the tea and took a good-sized swig from it. As soon as she swallowed the tea, she waved her other arm at the TV. "So, when did they announce it?"

"Right before I called you. I'm blown away. He always seemed like such a nice guy."

"You're right. I do their yard, but I've only seen him in passing a few times. He was always pleasant enough, but his wife could be a bit stuck up. I didn't have much to do with her, either, but I heard she hung around with Rita a lot. From the local gossip, I understand that Rita had a bad habit of crashing with them whenever she and Butch had a fight or she got drunk. I'm sure Ed was sick of that. He might actually find prison peaceful compared to the drama of living in his old situation."

Joni laughed, and then put her hand over her mouth as if to stifle it. "Oh my, I shouldn't be laughing about this. That poor man."

The news came back on with another breaking news update. This time they showed Ed Blake's mug shot—a middle-class looking man in a polo shirt, his short beard and hair neatly groomed. The announcer said he'd turned himself in and confessed to murdering Rita Grayson, whose body had been found in the Leisure Lakes clubhouse lake recently. The motive for the murder was not released.

Jess put the tea down and sat back in her chair. "Well, what do you know..."

"I know, right? Pretty amazing. Who would've guessed it was him? I bet his wife had no idea."

"I'm sure she didn't. Right now, I'm sure Kathy's happy she lives in a gated community, because the press would be camped out in her front yard, otherwise."

"Oh, goodness! That's right. I wonder if they've had to put an extra guard on the front gate?"

Chapter Thirty-two

"I CAN'T BELIEVE IT'S over at last," Beth said, putting her bare feet up on Jess' wicker coffee table. "It felt like this case was going nowhere and then bang! It was over, with four people trying to take credit for killing Rita. Who'd have imagined that?"

Jess raised her glass and clinked it with Beth's. "I know. I can't believe Ed did it. I was so afraid it was going to be Gabby. Did she ever say why she confessed?"

"When I nailed her down with Ed's confession, she finally told me she confessed because Rita had already hurt too many people. Gabby said she and Kathy weren't buddies, not even close at all. When she saw Rita turn on her only real friend that was the last straw. She decided Rita had done enough damage, and she was ready to 'take her out,' as she put it, if she couldn't scare her enough. When Ed came out and took the bat from her, she tried to get him to let her take care of the situation. Ed wouldn't let her. He told her to leave, but she didn't right away. She saw him take a swing at Rita with her bat before she left. She knew Ed had killed her when he didn't return her bat and Rita turned up dead. She assumed he'd thrown her bat in the lake because that's what she would've done."

"Okay, that means she knew who killed Rita, but not why she confessed."

"She told me Ed and Kathy had been through so much with Rita, and they deserved to be happy. Besides, Gabby told me she's older than Ed, and she's had a good life. She felt Ed and Kathy should have their life back, and she figured she could withstand the time in jail. She didn't think Ed should have to pay for what she'd been willing to do. She was sure Ed wouldn't have killed Rita if he hadn't stopped her from doing it. In other words, she thought she put the idea in his head."

Jess put her glass down and leaned back in her chair. "That's an amazing story. She was willing to take the blame for someone else so they could go on with their lives. I'm glad Ed did confess. It would've nagged at him for the rest of his life if he hadn't. That alone could've ruined their marriage, too."

Beth's head did a slow nod. "Kind of like Edgar Allan Poe's short story, 'The Telltale Heart.'"

"Exactly. Since Ed was the kind of guy who turned himself in, he would also have been the kind of guy who couldn't have let someone else take the blame for what he did. Was that what happened? The other question is how those people found out Gabby was confessing."

"The night before I went to talk to her that last time, she made a couple of calls to make sure the golf league was taken care of. After that, she called her best friends to let them know what was about to happen so they would hear the full story from her instead of seeing it on the news. It didn't take long at all before the story was all over Leisure Lakes. That's how Ed found out."

Jess picked up her glass and raised it in a salute. "The gossip connection strikes again."

"Exactly. The next question is whether he would've confessed if no one had been targeted for arrest. This thing could've gone unsolved, I guess, if I hadn't decided to talk to Gabby again."

"Possibly. By the way, I heard they practically threw Gabby a parade when the word got out that she had tried to get rid of Rita. I think everyone feels sorry for Ed, and they understand why he did it. He's a hero in their eyes, too. It's rare that a killer is also a kind of hero."

"I wonder what Kathy will do now. She's a victim too, in a way. Her husband will go to prison, and at his age, he may never come out. Rita's gaggle of friends will break up without its leader, so Kathy will be on her own except for her buddies that stick with her. Do you think she'll stay at Leisure Lakes?"

"Never know. Why do you ask?"

Beth grinned. "Just curious. I loved what I saw of their house. Kathy said if they ever decided to sell..."

Jess started laughing. "Seriously? You'd move to Leisure Lakes?"

"Maybe. If I could negotiate a good price for that place. I'm in love with their yard."

"They do have a beautiful yard. Of course, I'm a little prejudiced since I'm the one that takes care of it. Oh, no...you could become one of my customers!"

Beth furrowed her eyebrows and looked intently at Jess. "Hmm...would that make me sort of your boss?"

Jess shook her head as she chuckled, then answered quickly, "I. Don't. Think. So. I'm my own boss. Those people are my customers. Some are friends, but all of them are customers. I always reserve the right to tell them to find someone else if I don't like them or their yard.

Do you think I'd like you as a customer?"

Beth raised her eyebrows and grinned again. "I sure hope so. Anyway, that's conjecture. Kathy may decide to stick it out among people who know her. If she moves, she'll have to start over somewhere else, just to become the object of even more gossip."

"For now anyway, you've got a cute little apartment and don't have to go anywhere unless you want to." She leaned forward and reached for Beth's hand. "Besides, you can always come over here and sit on my porch any old time you like."

"That's a great invitation. Do you really mean it?"

Jess gave Beth's hand a little squeeze. "I do. I've decided I like having you around."

The End

About BJ Phillips

I've been writing practically since I've been reading. People who knew me well knew my biggest dream and biggest fear was writing a whole book. That fear of failure. I had poetry published in my school literary magazine and a funny story in my work professional magazine. I wrote training materials for work and helped friends write their resumes, feeling that was at least writing. I had the beginnings of fantasy stories, mysteries, and love stories all sitting in folders and notebooks.

In the summer of 2013, I saw the National Novel Writing Month (NaNoWriMo) challenge. If you're not familiar with it, the challenge is to write 50,000 words in 30 days. The day after Thanksgiving that year, I posted 51,000 words and a complete story was born. It needed a lot of work, but it was there. That story was the bones of Hurricane Season, my debut novel, which was published June 2016.

Early in 2014, I heard about a new program through the Golden Crown Literary Society (GCLS) called the Writing Academy. It's a one-year program aimed at new writers or writers who want to improve their skills. I'm proud to be part of the very first graduating class.

The Writing Academy was life changing. I started looking at myself as an author, not just as someone who happens to write. I retired at the beginning of 2015. I became a full-time writer of stories and finally finished my first book at the end of July 2015. Hurricane Season was followed by two more romances, Snowbird Season and Changing Seasons. Murder at Leisure Lakes is my first mystery.

I live in Florida with my partner, who is a retired police officer, and Maya the Yorkie in an honest-to-goodness resort—it says so on the sign out front. When I'm not writing, we love sitting out on the front porch with our little girl and chatting with neighbors and friends who like to come by and visit. I'm an avid reader of anything that strikes my fancy and I love puzzles – like logic problems, Sudoku or word finds. I also like to take walks, go to flea markets, sketch, and crochet. Okay, I'm also addicted to several TV shows, mostly mysteries and cop shows. Thank goodness for the DVR!

I'm very happy to be part of the Desert Palm Press family. I am working on another murder mystery right now.

Connect with BJ

Email: bjphillipswrites@gmail.com

Website: http://www.bjphillipsauthor.com/:

Note to Readers:

Thank you for reading a book from Desert Palm Press. We have made every effort to edit this book. However, typos do slip in. If you find an error in the text, please email lee@desertpalmpress.com so the issue can be corrected.

We appreciate you as a reader and want to ensure you enjoy the reading process. We would like you to consider posting a review on your preferred media sites and/or your blog or website.

For more information on upcoming releases, author interviews, contest, giveaways and more, please sign up for our newsletter and visit us as at Desert Palm Press: www.desertpalmpress.com and "Like" us on Facebook: Desert Palm Press.

Bright Blessings

Desert Palm Press

www.ingramcontent.com/pod-product-compliance
Lightning Source LLC
LaVergne TN
LVHW090958080826
845145LV00003B/1047

* 9 7 8 1 9 4 8 3 2 7 8 5 5 *